Sheila Norton lives near Chelmsford in Essex with her husband, and worked for most of her life as a medical secretary, before retiring early to concentrate on her writing. Sheila is the award-winning writer of numerous women's fiction novels and over 100 short stories, published in women's magazines. She has three married daughters, six little grandchildren, and over the years has enjoyed the companionship of three cats and two dogs. She derived lots of inspiration for her books *Oliver the Cat Who Saved Christmas* and *Charlie the Kitten Who Saved a Life* from remembering the pleasure and fun of sharing life with her own cats. Sheila is convinced cats can understand Human and that we really ought to learn to speak Cat!

When not working on her writing Sheila enjoys spending time with her family and friends, as well as reading, walking, swimming, photography and travel. For more information visit www.sheilanorton.com

SHEILA NORTON

CHARLIE
THE KITTEN WHO SAVED A LIFE

EBURY
PRESS

1 3 5 7 9 10 8 6 4 2

Ebury Press, an imprint of Ebury Publishing
20 Vauxhall Bridge Road,
London SW1V 2SA

Penguin
Random House
UK

Ebury Press is part of the Penguin Random House group of companies
whose addresses can be found at global.penguinrandomhouse.com

Copyright © Sheila Norton, 2016

Sheila Norton has asserted her right to be identified as the author of this
work in accordance with the Copyright, Designs and Patents Act 1988

First published in 2016 by Ebury Press

www.penguin.co.uk

A CIP catalogue record for this book is available from the British Library

ISBN 9781785034190

Printed and bound in Great Britain by Clays Ltd, St Ives PLC

Penguin Random House is committed to a sustainable future
for our business, our readers and our planet. This book is made from
Forest Stewardship Council® certified paper.

For my lovely family – including their cats!

CHARLIE

THE KITTEN WHO SAVED A LIFE

TRANSLATED FROM
'KITTEN' BY
SHEILA NORTON

CHAPTER
ONE

OK, settle down, you lot. My friend Oliver here says you're all desperate to hear my story, so please come out from behind the dustbins for a minute and stop fighting over that dead sparrow. Now, before we start, I know that some of you still think of me as a silly little tabby kitten who barely knows his tail from his whiskers, but I've had to grow up a lot during this summer, and you'll understand why when you hear my story. Oliver, could you let my sisters sit next to you in case they get frightened? That's right, Nancy. Yes, snuggle up to Oliver, Tabitha. I do feel a bit protective of you both, you see, even though we spend our lives living with separate human families. And if there are any *really* little kittens listening, or any scaredy-cats – sorry, I mean any cats of a nervous disposition – you may need to cover your ears with your paws at certain parts. No, Tabitha, I didn't mean *yet*. I haven't even started. I'll tell you when we get to a scary part.

Where should I begin? Well, I suppose I should start with the day I found out about the holiday. Of course, back then, before it all happened, I had no idea what a holiday was. The first I heard about it was when my human, Julian, came home from work one evening and announced:

'Right. I've booked a holiday.'

His female, Laura, just looked up at him, her eyes all cloudy with tiredness. I felt sorry for her, because I knew she hadn't been getting much sleep. None of us had.

'Oh, Julian,' she said, sighing. 'It's a nice idea, but how on earth can we go on holiday at the moment? With all the bits and pieces we'd need to take for the baby?'

Right on cue, the baby, Jessica, who was upstairs in her little white basket, supposedly asleep, began to mew at the top of her voice. You know the sweet, soft little squeaky noises we make when we're new-born kittens? Well, trust me, this was nothing like it. Human kittens, as I'd now learned only too well, make the most terrible din you can imagine. They howl. Their little faces go red, their mouths open so wide they seem to fill their whole face, and they scream. It happens when they want milk, but it also seems to happen for no apparent reason, any time, day or night. No wonder poor Laura looked exhausted.

'I'll go,' Julian said, throwing his jacket on a chair and heading up the stairs. I trotted up after him. He hadn't said hello to me yet. I meowed at him a bit and jumped round his feet while he lifted Jessica out of her basket, but he just said, 'Mind out of the way, Charlie. I don't want to drop the baby.'

The baby, the baby. It was all I heard about, these days! I mean, she was cute, I supposed, when she wasn't yelling, but what about me? I wasn't getting my share of cuddles anymore, and there had even been times when they'd forgotten all about my dinner. I'd had to walk round and round my empty dish so many times, calling for attention, I ended up getting dizzy.

Still ignoring me, Julian carried the baby out of the little pink room where she slept and past the door of Caroline's bedroom. Caroline, our big human kitten, had had what her father called a *growth spurt* recently. If she'd been a cat, I'd have said she was more or less fully grown, but humans seem to stay kittens for much longer than we do. She spent a lot of time in her bedroom, especially since the baby had arrived. I sneaked in there with her as often as I could. She was the only one who still seemed to have time to cuddle me.

'Hello, Caroline!' Julian called out, pausing outside her door and tapping on it gently. 'Come downstairs, I've got something exciting to tell you.'

I waited for her outside her door, and after a bit she came out and trudged down the stairs alongside me.

'What is it?' she asked. She didn't look like someone who was about to be told something exciting. In fact Julian was the only one looking remotely excited. As usual, nobody was telling *me* what was going on so I just had to listen carefully to their Human chat and try to pick up some clues.

'I've booked us a holiday,' Julian said again. He smiled, obviously pleased with himself. He'd been standing jiggling the squawking baby in his arms, and now he placed her on Laura's lap so that she could feed her.

'Oh, cool!' Caroline said, brightening up. 'Where are we going? Is it Florida? One of the girls at school went there last year.'

'Florida?' Julian echoed, staring at her. 'No, of course not. We can't go somewhere like that with a three-month-old baby.'

'Oh.' Caroline's mouth turned down again. 'Typical. Everything's about *her* now.'

'Caroline!' Julian said, giving her a warning look. 'That's not true, at all—'

'So, where are we going?' she interrupted.

'Mudditon-on-Sea.'

There was silence. Even baby Jessica was quiet now she was being fed. Caroline just stared back at her father, while Laura shook her head as if she couldn't quite believe it.

'But it'll be lovely!' Julian said, looking from one of them to the other. 'I've booked us a beautiful holiday cottage for the whole of August.'

'The whole of August?' Caroline gasped.

'Yes! Look,' he said, turning to Laura, 'I know how hard it's been for you. The pregnancy wasn't easy, the Caesarean left you exhausted, and the baby's been hard work—'

'How can you possibly take a whole month off?' Laura said.

'Oh.' Julian sat down next to her, his smile fading. 'Well, I'm not, exactly. I'll just spend the first week with you all, then of course I'll have to come back.'

'And go back to work.'

'Yes, but I'll come down for weekends. You can enjoy the sea air, darling, and get lots of rest.'

'Rest? In a self-catering cottage?' she said quietly. 'I'll still have to do everything, Julian, the baby won't stop being demanding just because we're at the seaside, and you won't even be there to help.'

'And *I'm* not coming!' Caroline said, her face all red and cross. 'I don't want to spend the whole school holiday at boring Mudditon-on-Sea. My friends are all planning stuff. Going into town on the bus and going to the cinema and things, and I'll be the only one not around!'

With which she stomped back upstairs and slammed her bedroom door.

Julian got to his feet, looking upset.

'Leave her,' Laura said. 'She'll come round.'

'I'm sorry,' he said, spreading his paws out helplessly. 'I've got it all wrong, haven't I? I'd better cancel it.'

'No, don't.' She looked up at him now, smiling. 'Sorry I wasn't more excited, love. I'm just so tired, I can't think straight.'

'I thought it'd be a nice surprise. We all need a break. Things have been so tense recently. I'm worried about Caroline, she's looking pale and sad all the time, and she keeps shutting herself away upstairs. I thought the sea air would do everyone some good.'

'I know. It *is* a nice idea. I'm sure we'll have fun.'

Her smile looked a bit strange, like she didn't really mean it. Julian went upstairs again to get changed, and I jumped up on the sofa next to her. She looked at me over the top of the baby's head.

'Not *really* my idea of fun, Charlie,' she whispered. 'On my own with a crying baby and a sulky girl who doesn't want to come. But what can I do? I don't want to hurt his feelings.'

I meowed back at her and she took one hand away from the baby to pat me gently on the head. But like all humans,

7

she didn't understand Cat, so she didn't know I was trying to say something very important to her: *'What about me? Who's going to look after me while you're away? Doesn't anyone think about me anymore?'*

The next day, when Julian had gone to work and Caroline was at school, Laura's friend Nicky came round with her baby, Benjamin. Benjamin was a lot bigger than our Jessica, and was now managing to stand on his back paws and do a funny sort of walk for a few steps before he fell over. It beats me why humans bother with all that effort of walking on two paws. What's the point? I've tried it, several times, but it just doesn't work. It seems like the most unnatural thing in the world.

I liked Nicky. She always made a fuss of me, playing with me and scratching me on the head and under the chin just the way I like, making me purr with pleasure.

'So, is Caroline excited about it?' Nicky asked when Laura had finished telling her about the holiday.

'No. She's not happy at all.' Laura sighed, shaking her head. 'She told Julian she doesn't want to come and she's hardly spoken a word to either of us since. She's gone off to school in a huff this morning.'

'Well, I suppose a whole month *is* a long time. She'll probably miss her friends. She's getting to an age where her friends are just as important to her as her family.'

'I know. And of course, she's already cross enough about September when she's going to a different school from her friends in the village. I really hope we're doing the right thing, Nicky, sending her to the private school. It's been so nice seeing how she's made friends now, after all that time off being so lonely while she was ill.'

That was before I came to live with them, but I knew all about it from Oliver, because he used to visit the family before I was born. Caroline had been very poorly, and apparently Laura had been her nurse until Julian decided he wanted her as his female.

'She'll come round. She'll make new friends easily enough once she starts at St Margaret's,' Nicky said, and Laura sighed again.

'I do hope so. We're quite worried about her, to be honest. She seems so tired and listless all the time these days. Almost everything I say, she snaps my head off. I asked her to tidy her room a few days ago and she said *"You can't tell me what to do, you're not my mother."*'

'Oh dear. That must have been hurtful.'

'Well, I guess she must still think about her mum. It's only natural, even though Caroline was quite little when she died. I've never tried to take her place.'

'I know. And she does love you really, Laura. Perhaps she's just feeling tired. It's the end of term – all the kids are probably ready for a break.'

'Yes, that's true. Anyway she's got her check-up at the hospital next week. We're going to ask her consultant to run some tests.'

'Really? You're that worried?' Nicky took hold of Laura's paw. 'You don't think the leukaemia has come back?'

'That's what we're frightened of, obviously,' Laura said quietly. 'It's hard not to fear the worst. She's only been in remission for a year.'

Nicky put her arm round Laura. I could tell I wasn't going to get stroked anymore so I jumped down and ran off to play outside. As you know, my house is the one they call The Big House, so I have a lot of lovely grounds within my territory, a lot of borders to patrol to make sure none of you lot sneak in without my permission. It's quite a responsibility. It was a lovely warm day, with all sorts of wonderful scents in the air, and dopy insects and birds out of their trees and bushes, so I was having fun jumping around, chasing my shadow in the sunshine, and I must have been gone longer than I thought.

When I finally returned, they were all home. And to my disgust, nobody took the slightest notice of me again, because there was another argument going on.

'I can't *believe* you're going to do that!' Caroline was saying crossly to her father. 'How *could* you? He'll hate it!'

'No he won't,' Julian said. 'It'll be like a holiday for him.'

Oh, more talk about holidays. I didn't want to hear it. I just wanted my dinner. I meowed loudly at them all, walking around them and flicking my tail.

Laura looked down at me, frowning.

'Perhaps I could ask Nicky if she and Dan could look after him,' she said. 'Although it *is* a whole month. It's a bit much.'

I stopped meowing abruptly. Were they talking about *me*?

'No. I've said, he can go to the cattery,' Julian said. 'He'll be fine.'

The cattery? I felt my fur begin to stand on end. Oliver had told me about that place. I'll never forget the story, it's haunted me ever since. You really want to hear it, Nancy? Well, it was apparently our father – Oliver's friend Tabby – who was sent to the cattery once, when his humans went away. He said it was the worst experience of his nine lives. He was kept in a cage, day and night, with just a bed and a litter tray. And although there were lots of other cats there, he couldn't see them, he just smelt their fear and heard them crying. He wasn't allowed out to hunt, and although he was fed regularly he felt too stressed to eat much. Apparently the humans who looked after him there were friendly, and gave him plenty of strokes and cuddles, but he didn't know whether to trust them or not, and had no idea whether he was ever going home again. He had nothing in the cage that smelt of home or his humans, and by the time they finally came back to collect him he was so upset he wouldn't have anything to do with them for days – he went off on his own and they thought he'd run away. Of course, eventually he gave in because he was so hungry, but Oliver said it took him a long time to get over it.

Yes, it's a horrible story, isn't it? So, as you can imagine, when I heard the cattery being mentioned, I let out a long, mournful cry of distress. Caroline dived on me and picked me up, holding me tight. Her eyes looked all wet.

'That's just *great*,' she said, although I didn't think it was, at all. 'Not only are you taking me away from all my friends for a *whole month*, just before I have to say goodbye to them forever to go to that stupid new school – but now you're even taking my cat away from me! It's so unfair!'

I agreed. It was. I didn't want to go to the cattery. I wondered if I should run away before they took me there. Caroline started to cry, and I joined in.

'Oh, for heaven's sake,' said Julian. 'What do you want me to do? We can't take him with us.'

'Can't we?' Laura said quietly. She put a paw on Julian's arm. 'It might be a better option.'

'How?' he demanded. 'You can't just take a cat to a strange place. He'll run off and get lost. Is that what you want?' he asked, turning to Caroline.

'No!' she said. 'I don't want *any* of it! I don't want to come! I'll stay at home with Charlie.'

'Julian, I'm sure we could manage it,' Laura said. 'He's been neutered, so he's not so likely to stray.'

'But we'd still have to keep all the doors and windows shut the whole time – and in summer too! It's just not realistic. He'll get out and get lost.'

'We'll have to make sure he doesn't.'

Laura and Julian were looking at each other. I could tell they were more worried about Caroline being upset than about me suffering the stress of the cattery, but just thinking about being shut in one of those cages, I let out another loud yowl of distress and finally Julian gave a little laugh – the type that sounded like he wasn't really amused – and said:

'All right, all right. I give in. We'll take him with us.' He turned to Caroline again. 'But you'll have to play your part in keeping him safe.'

'I will,' she said. She nuzzled my head with her cheek and I purred happily. Thank goodness. No cage. 'I will, because Charlie's the only one around here who cares about me.'

With which she carried me upstairs to her room and we lay on her bed together.

So it seemed like I was going on holiday, whatever that meant. I'd have preferred to stay here and play with my friend Oliver. But I never get a say in anything!

CHAPTER
TWO

I had mixed feelings about baby Jessica. When they first brought her into the house, everyone, even Caroline, was ridiculously excited about her, but I didn't seem to be allowed anywhere near her.

'Keep Charlie away from her,' Laura said on the very first day they brought her home. 'You hear terrible things about cats and new babies.'

I felt quite upset by this. I mean, it was true I didn't like her constant high-pitched mewing, but I'd never have done anything to hurt her – she was only a tiny human kitten. Sometimes she smelt nice and milky, but at other times, when Laura or Julian were doing things with her bottom that made me feel violently ill, I didn't want to be anywhere near her. I hoped it wouldn't be long before they trained her to use a litter tray. Because of Jessica, I started being shut in the kitchen quite often, and if I protested by meowing loudly about it, I got told off. That seemed quite unfair because nobody told the baby off for crying, and I think she was louder than me.

By the time the holiday was being discussed, I suppose I was getting used to the situation. But Caroline's excitement about having a baby sister had completely worn off. That day after the argument about the cattery, she poured out her heart to me as we lay on her bed together.

'I'm fed up with it, Charlie. I can't imagine why I was looking forward to the new baby coming. Daddy's never got time for me now. I feel like I'm just in the way.'

I knew how she felt. Only the previous day I'd been shouted at for bringing a nice fat woodpigeon in through the cat flap. I thought they'd be proud of me, as it was the biggest one I'd ever caught, but oh no, there was a lot of squawking and carrying on about *germs* and *the baby*, and Laura shooed me back outside while she got rid of my prize trophy.

'At least they're not saying you're a danger to the baby and shutting you out in case you attack her,' I pointed out to Caroline now, in Cat, but of course, she still hadn't bothered to learn our language so she just stroked me and nuzzled the top of my head.

'And as for this *holiday!*' she went on crossly. 'It's going to be awful! Thank goodness Daddy's finally agreed to let you come with us. At least I'll have you to keep me company. I'm going to go mad, stuck in some boring place with no friends, for a *whole month*.'

Listening to Caroline's complaints, I must admit I was beginning to feel quite anxious about this holiday thing. Nobody apart from Julian seemed to think it was a good idea, and even he was getting stressed whenever it was mentioned. I wondered whether my humans were ever going to start being happy and cheerful again like they used to be.

One day soon afterwards, I was sitting on the kitchen windowsill washing my whiskers after my dinner when I heard raised voices again in the dining room.

'Eat your dinner, Caroline,' Julian was saying.

'Don't want it.'

'What's wrong with it?' Laura said. 'You've always liked spaghetti bolognese.'

'Well, I don't now!' Caroline sounded like she might be going to cry. 'I keep telling you, I don't like meat anymore. I'm not hungry.'

'You're hungry enough when it comes to biscuits and sweets!' Laura retorted. 'We'll have to stop all those treats if you can't eat your dinners.'

'You'll make yourself ill if you don't eat properly,' Julian told her.

'Maybe I *am* ill!' Caroline said. 'Maybe I've got the leukaemia again. Not that you'd care!'

I'd stopped washing, sitting very still while I listened to all of this. I didn't like to think that Caroline might be ill again. I don't think Julian or Laura liked it either, because after she'd gone off upstairs to her bedroom again, they were talking very quietly together about her hospital appointment in London the following day. Apparently Julian was taking her there instead of going to work, and he and Laura both sounded worried about it.

'Some of the symptoms are just the same as before,' Julian said. 'The tiredness, pallor, loss of appetite...'

'But she's so *cross* all the time, too!' Laura said. 'I can't seem to get through to her anymore. I know she's worried about starting the new school. Do you think it's that?'

'Surely not. She'll soon settle there when she starts. No, I think she's probably as frightened as we are, about the thought of being ill again. That's why she's being so snappy. We should try to be understanding.'

'Well, I'm glad you're seeing the consultant tomorrow. Let's hope he can reassure us.'

They went off early in the morning in Julian's car to catch the train from Great Broomford. I hung around indoors for a while, thinking Laura and Jessica might like my company. I'd found an old toy mouse of mine behind my bed, and after I'd got bored with playing with it on my own in the kitchen, I thought it might be nice to let Jessica have a turn with it. I trotted into the lounge with it in my mouth. Laura was sitting in one of the armchairs, reading the paper, so she didn't see me come in, and Jessica was lying on a blanket on the floor, staring at the ceiling and making funny little noises as she kicked her back paws in the air. I dropped the toy mouse onto her face and waited to see if she'd realise she was supposed to play with it, but her eyes went wide with surprise and she shook her head so that it fell off onto the blanket next to her. I sat down next to her head and waited. She smelt nice and clean and I quite fancied lying down with her and seeing if she'd stroke me. But just then, Laura turned a page of her paper and glanced down at the baby.

'Charlie!' she said, throwing the paper down. 'What are you doing?'

'Looking after Jessica,' I meowed. Wasn't it obvious?

'Get away from the baby's face,' she said. 'And ... what on earth is *that*?' She bent down and picked up my toy mouse. 'What is this revolting dirty old thing doing in here? I don't want it on Jessica's blanket!' She picked it up and sighed at me. 'Honestly, I can't take my eyes off her for one single minute while you're around, can I?'

I ran off to hide behind the sofa while she fussed around with the baby, straightening out the blanket and moving it even closer to her chair, as if to protect her from me. I couldn't see what I'd done wrong. It wasn't as if it was a *real* mouse. Or perhaps that was what she'd prefer? I decided to try that next time.

From behind the sofa, I watched Laura with the newspaper for a while. I loved the rustling noise it made when she turned the pages, and one of my favourite things was to jump up on her lap, on top of the paper, so that I could tread all over it, scrunching it with my paws. She used to laugh when I did that, but these days she just sighed loudly and lifted me off her, so there wasn't much point. But when Jessica started to cry and Laura laid the paper down on the floor to pick her up, I couldn't resist it any longer. I dived across the room, jumped on the outspread pages and had a lovely time walking round in circles, making satisfying scrunching sounds.

'Charlie!' she snapped, sounding really cross this time. 'Get off! What on *earth* is the matter with you these days?'

I yowled in protest as she pushed me off the paper and put it back on the arm of her chair. It looked a bit torn but I knew she got a new one every day so I couldn't see why it was such a big deal.

'Go and play outside,' she told me as she sat down to feed Jessica. 'I really can't cope with you being difficult at the moment.'

Me, difficult? I went out, feeling hurt and unloved. If that was how she felt, I wouldn't bother hunting for a mouse for baby Jessica after all. So there!

Julian and Caroline were home when I came back into the kitchen later. Caroline had gone into the lounge to watch the TV.

'The consultant sent us to have blood samples taken for testing, and if the result is suspicious of the illness returning, she'll have to have a bone marrow biopsy,' Julian was telling Laura.

'Oh no. Not again. Poor Caroline,' Laura said. 'Did he say he thinks it *is* the leukaemia?'

'He wouldn't say. He said her symptoms might just as easily be something else, but of course with her history he wants to rule it out.' Julian sighed. 'He did say the blood test results might not be back with the GP for a while, though.'

'And we're supposed to be going away tomorrow. Do you want to wait until we get the results? It wouldn't hurt to put off going for a few days.'

I thought Laura actually sounded quite cheerful about the idea. But Julian shook his head.

'No. The results might take longer than that, and anyway I can phone for them from Mudditon.'

'But if she *does* need the biopsy . . .'

'Laura, I'm trying to be positive here! I think we should go ahead as planned. Caroline needs this holiday as much as we do. The sea air will do her good. If she does have to have the biopsy, I'll just have to bring her back for a few days.'

'OK.' Laura put her paws round Julian's middle. 'You're right, we mustn't keep thinking the worst.'

'Hard not to, though.' He sighed. 'Well, hopefully the holiday will help take our minds off it.'

The next morning, everyone was up before me. Jessica had, as usual, woken me up during the night so I'd decided to go out for a moonlight stroll. You know how pleasant it is, on a summer's evening, to scamper around outside in the dark, when most of the humans are asleep. Having such good night vision is a wonderful thing! I like trying to catch little field mice and voles unawares on nights like that. I was having such fun, I didn't stop at the boundary of my own territory but carried on chasing one little mouse all the way down the lane into the centre of Little Broomford village. Suddenly a bigger cat loomed out of the darkness in front of me, making me skid to a stop, stifling a whimper of fright. I shouldn't have wandered this far at night – I was probably trespassing in someone else's territory and might have been about to get told off, or worse, attacked, for my cheek.

'Charlie, it's me!' the bigger cat meowed, just as I was about to make a run for it.

'Oh, hello, Ollie!' I felt a bit embarrassed, then, for behaving like a scaredy-cat. But he came up to me and rubbed his face against mine.

'It's brave of you, isn't it, being out in the village on your own at this time of night?'

I was still a little kitten to Oliver, you see. He's always been protective of me.

'It's such a nice night for hunting,' I explained. 'I was chasing a mouse, and I got carried away.'

'Well, let's go back up the lane together. How are you – I haven't seen you for a few days.'

'I know. To be honest, so much has been happening at home, with my humans, I've been so worried … I hardly know where to start.'

'What's wrong? Are they in trouble?'

'I don't know. I can't work it out – you know how complicated humans are. They're all really stressed and cross with each other—'

'Well, you've been saying that since the new kitten – Jessica – arrived, haven't you?'

'Yes, but it's got even worse lately. It's Caroline I'm most worried about. She seems so unhappy, a lot of the time. I know Julian and Laura are worried about her too. You don't think she's got that horrible illness again, do you, Ollie?'

'I certainly hope not. It was so good to see her getting better, I'd hate to think of her being ill again. Is that what Julian and Laura think, then?'

'They seem to, yes. Julian took her somewhere today to see a *consultant*, and he looked very worried when they came back. I wish I knew what I could do to make her better.'

'It's really hard to know how to help humans, some-times,' Oliver said seriously. And he should know. As you're all aware, he's famous for having helped everyone in the whole village, back before I was born. 'You need to listen carefully to their conversations and try to pick up clues.'

'All they do is argue, these days,' I said sadly. 'And a lot of the rows are about the holiday.'

'Oh yes, you told me about that. It means they're going away somewhere, right? And have they decided yet what's happening to you? Not the cattery, I hope?' he added with a shudder.

'No. They say they're taking me with them. I'm a bit nervous about it, though, as I don't really understand where we're going, or why. Nobody seems to be looking forward to it. But at least I'll be with Caroline. I'm sure she'll look after me. I only wish I could make her happy.'

'Try taking a nice fat mouse back for her tonight?' Oliver suggested.

'Laura would go mad. She keeps telling me off about things like that. She seems to think they're dirty.'

'Yes, it's odd how humans aren't always pleased with our gifts. But surely Caroline would be grateful, at least?'

'I could try it,' I said doubtfully. 'But I think she might just prefer a cuddle, to be honest.'

'That's the best thing,' Ollie agreed. 'Humans always like cuddling us. They think they're doing it for our sakes, but of course, it's really the other way around. They're very needy creatures, you know, Charlie. Very fragile, emotionally. It's a good thing we cats are so well-balanced or we'd never be able to cope with them.'

I said goodbye to Ollie at the gates of my house and went wearily in to bed, our conversation still playing on my mind. After such a late night, I'd have appreciated a lie-in in the morning, but it wasn't to be. Julian and Laura were up, dressed, and rushing around the house like cats being chased by foxes. They were folding clothes, picking up things and putting them in bags, calling to Caroline to get herself ready. I felt quite left out of it all, and was rather grumpy about having had to remind them three times about my breakfast. Then I noticed they'd left one suitcase open in their bedroom, with some nice soft clothes of Laura's right on top. Well, it was as good a place as any to settle down for a nap and try to catch up on my sleep. I made a nice little nest for myself in a soft cardigan and pulled a dress over the top of me, and was just dozing off when Julian marched into the room again calling out to Laura:

'Is this case finished? Can I close it up now?', before slinging the lid of the suitcase down on top of me.

'Help! Let me out!' I meowed in panic – and the lid was opened again and the dress lifted off me.

'Charlie!' Julian said, and I wasn't sure from his tone of voice whether he was cross or amused. 'What on earth are you doing in there?' He lifted me out onto the floor, just as Laura came into the room behind him. 'Charlie was having a nap in the suitcase!' he told her.

'Well, I hope he hasn't creased my new dress,' she said.

I noticed Julian having a quick look at the dress, frowning and glancing at me before he closed the lid in a hurry and fastened up the case.

'I'm sure it'll be fine,' he said. And then, to my absolute horror, he went outside to the garage and came back in with the dreaded Carrying Basket.

'But I thought you said I wasn't going to the cattery!' I yelled.

They'd lied! How could they do this to me? I made a dash for the cat flap but even more horror – it was locked! There was no escape!

'Sorry, Charlie,' Laura said, picking me up and giving me a stroke. 'But you'll have to spend the journey in your basket. It'll be fine. There you go.'

I tried to struggle, kicking my legs out so I couldn't fit through the opening, but Laura pushed me in and clipped the metal door shut.

I cried mournfully as she carried me outside in the basket and loaded me into the car. I was put on the floor, just under where baby Jessica was sitting in her funny little seat. From the gaps in the top of my basket I could just see her back paws in their little pink socks. Caroline got into the other side of the back seat and bent down to talk to me.

'Shush, Charlie, you're all right, don't cry. We're going on a long journey so perhaps you'll have a little sleep.'

It was only then that I realised I wasn't going to the cattery after all but being taken on the holiday. I was so relieved, I did actually stop crying for a while – which is more than I can say for Jessica.

CHAPTER
THREE

I hate being in a car. I don't suppose I'm the only one, am I? No, I didn't think so! For one thing, I've already learnt that it normally means we're going to the vet. Then there's the horrible noise cars make and the way they seem to quiver, as they go along, like a cat about to pounce on its prey. Even though I'd stopped crying, I couldn't help myself from letting out little whimpers of fear. Caroline kept talking to me, but eventually she was getting drowned out by the noise of Jessica's screaming.

'Can't I have Charlie sitting on my lap?' she called above the din to Laura.

'No. He might jump off and try to sit on top of Jessica.'

'I won't!' I mewed.

'He won't,' Caroline said. 'Oh, please let him. He's frightened. I'll hold onto him.'

'No, it's not safe,' Julian said. 'Anyway, it's the law – cats have to be in a carrier on car journeys. And if we had to stop suddenly he could get hurt.'

'Not fair,' I heard Caroline mutter to herself. 'Poor Charlie.'

So I closed my eyes, told myself sternly to stop being a scaredy-cat, and tried to settle down and catch up on the sleep I'd missed the previous night. It was getting hot in the car with the sunshine coming through the windows and I felt cramped and uncomfortable in my basket. As we all

31

know, even in extreme circumstances, sleep has to take priority. But have you ever tried to get to sleep with a human kitten wailing its head off just above you?

'Shush, Jessica,' Laura kept saying, turning round in her seat and trying to reach one of the baby's paws to stroke. 'All right, baby, all right.'

'What's the matter with her?' Caroline asked irritably.

'She's probably tired.'

'So why doesn't she just go to sleep?'

Good question.

'I don't know. Perhaps she's feeling unsettled because normally she'd be having a sleep in her cot or in the pram now. Babies don't like things being different.'

'Pity we didn't stay at home, then,' Caroline whispered in my direction.

'Why don't you talk to her, Caroline?' Laura suggested.

'What about?'

'Well, just try to calm her down. Give her hand a little stroke. Make sure she's got her dummy and her blankie.'

'Oh, great! Now I'm being used as a *child*minder! Is this how it's going to be on this holiday? Because if it is, I'm going out every day!'

'Caroline, don't talk to Laura like that,' Julian said. 'Please just give Jessica her dummy like you've been asked. Then perhaps we'll all get some peace.'

It took a while, but eventually Jessica's wailing died away and all I could hear was the funny sucking noise she made when that dummy thing was in her mouth. I often wondered what it tasted like and why, when she spent half the day sucking away at it, it never got any smaller. I quite fancied having a go with it, but they never left it anywhere where I could get it. Still, at least it was keeping her quiet. Caroline was quiet, too, apart from a faint tinny sort of noise, which I recognised as coming from the things she puts in her ears, connected to Julian's little screen thing he sometimes lets her play with. It often made her nod her head and tap her feet. Humans are weird, aren't they? If they're not putting bits and pieces in their mouths they're putting them in their ears. I don't know why they can't just leave themselves alone.

I finally managed to doze off, but a little bit later I woke up with a start. The car was standing still. Were we there, at the holiday? Could I come out of the basket now? I meowed loudly, just in case they were all going to get out and forget about me.

'It's OK, Charlie,' Caroline said. 'We're just having our picnic.'

Picnic? What on earth was a picnic? It's amazing how many words there must be in the Human language. Almost every day I hear another new one. I definitely think they have more words than we have in Cat, hard though that is to believe, but then again, they only speak with their voices, whereas of course we use our whole bodies as well. How else are they supposed to communicate all the signals we give with our tails? Humans don't even *have* tails! Or whiskers! And their ears don't even twitch. It doesn't bear thinking about.

I peered up through the top of my basket and could see Caroline in the back seat eating a sandwich. Well, it looked exactly like a sandwich but apparently *picnic* was a new name for it.

'Can I have some?' I meowed to her.

'Aw, Charlie's hungry,' she said. 'Can I give him some cheese? Can he come out and sit on my lap *now*?'

'All right, if you've finished eating,' Julian agreed. 'Just while we've stopped. He'll have to go back when we go to use the conveniences though.' *Conveniences*. Yet another new word. Where were they going to use them, and what was convenient about them? 'Are all the windows closed?' he added.

'Yes. And there are some cat treats in the bag,' Laura said. 'Give him some of those, and I've got some milk in a container here.'

That was more like it. Caroline undid the basket and lifted me out. Jessica's little seat was empty – she was on Laura's lap in the front, being fed. From the window I could see lots and lots of other cars, all lined up in rows, like they were having a meeting. I crunched up all my cat treats and lapped the milk out of the dish Laura had poured it into. I was feeling better now and ready for a run around. Also …

'I need a wee!' I meowed to Caroline.

'I've just thought,' she told Laura, as if she'd understood me. 'He's going to need a wee now he's had that milk.'

'Damn, I didn't think of that,' Julian said.

'I did,' Laura said calmly. 'I've got a portable litter tray. It's in the boot.'

So despite my complaints I was first put back into the basket 'for safety' while Julian opened the car door and went round to the boot – which some of you probably know, isn't a boot at all but part of the car. (When they have so many words to choose from, why do they use the name of a shoe to describe the back of a car?) And then, when he came back and the door was closed again, I was taken back *out* of the basket and pushed inside this *thing* they'd put on the back seat next to Caroline. I can only describe it as a cardboard box, with some of my toilet litter scattered inside, as if that was going to help! I couldn't believe my eyes. Were they joking? Did they seriously imagine any self-respecting cat was going to use *that* – in the car, with all of them watching? I'd rather die! And ... well, by the time we finally arrived at the holiday, with my bladder bursting, the baby yelling again, Caroline moaning about being bored and Julian snapping at her, you know what? I was thinking of giving up one of my nine lives voluntarily, if only I could be back at home in Little Broomford, playing in the grounds with Oliver or lying in my nice comfy bed!

'It's all right, Charlie,' Caroline was soothing me as she carried me, in my basket, into the strange place they were calling the Holiday Cottage. 'I'll let you out in a minute.'

While of course it was true I didn't like being in the basket, I was more concerned now about relieving myself before I burst, so I was grateful to see Laura was following her, carrying, among other things, my proper litter tray from home, the one I remembered using when I was very little, and then again after I came home from having that *operation* at the vet's. No grown-up cat likes using a litter tray if they have the option of a proper toilet in a flowerbed outside, of course, but the circumstances were now urgent. As soon as they'd shut the door and let me out of the basket, I zoomed across the room into my tray. And only then did I feel comfortable enough to take in my surroundings. Caroline had already gone off to explore the cottage, so I bounded after her so we could look around together. It didn't take long.

'It's *tiny*,' Caroline complained as we went back downstairs.

Julian laughed. 'You only think that because you've always lived in a big house. This is quite a decent size by normal standards.'

'There are only two bedrooms!'

'How many do you think we need?' Laura said. 'Daddy's right – we're very spoilt, at home. Your dad has worked hard all his life to afford the lovely home we have. But this cottage is so pretty, don't you think? It's obviously very old, but it's nice and cosy. And just look at the view from this window!' She put her paws around Julian. 'Well done, darling. It's a lovely choice.'

Caroline went to join them looking out of the window, and gasped, 'Oh! The sea is right *there*! It almost looks like we could jump into it from here!'

I leapt up onto the windowsill to see what was so exciting – and nearly fell off again with fright. Have any of you ever seen the sea? No? Well, I don't know how to begin to describe it to you. Try to picture that huge pond we've got in the grounds of the Big House. You know, Oliver, where you once told me that according to Cat legend, an ancient Siamese called Old Chalky fell in one day while being chased by a fox, and lost his ninth life. Now, imagine that pond being the size of the whole of Little Broomford. And not only that, it moves! It goes backwards and forwards, up and down, looking like it's going to come and get you. Needless to say, my first instinct was to run, but I fought the urge, because only a scaredy-cat leaves his human family to face danger on their own. So despite the trembling of my heart, I faced up to that horrible, threatening, moving thing beyond the window, arching my back and growling at it as fiercely as I could. Not that it took any notice – it just kept on coming.

Caroline and Laura were both laughing. How could they find this so amusing?

'Charlie, you funny little cat, it's the sea!' Caroline said, picking me up and, to my horror, holding me right against the window. 'It won't hurt you!'

'He's never seen it before, and cats don't like water,' Laura said. 'Put him down, he's struggling.'

I was. I couldn't understand why none of them seemed bothered about the fact that there was only this thin bit of glass between us and disaster.

'This is another reason why we must make sure he doesn't get out of the cottage,' Julian warned.

'Oh, don't worry!' I meowed as I ran off to find out where my bed had been put. 'I'm not getting any closer to that *sea* thing than I can help, thank you very much!'

Thankfully, the kitchen, where they'd put my bed, felt nice and safe. Its window, as I discovered when I plucked up the courage to jump up and investigate, looked out over the garden instead of the sea. The garden looked very small. I could see a wall going all the way round it, not a particularly high wall, so there was definitely a danger that we could be prone to illegal visits from strange cats who didn't realise this was now my territory. I puzzled for a while over how I was supposed to defend the garden if I wasn't going to be allowed outside. I doubted whether growling from the windowsill was going to have any more effect on a feline interloper than it did on the sea. This was a worry, but I'd have to face it when it happened. Meanwhile I was pleased to see my dinner had been dished up and was waiting for me in my bowl, and after eating this and having a good wash, I felt a bit more settled. I joined the family back in the living room, averting my eyes from the big window. The sea still hadn't come through into the room, so perhaps it had given up. I jumped up on Caroline's lap and she stroked me nicely while she watched TV, and needless to say I eventually dozed off.

When I woke up, I was lying in one of the armchairs – Caroline must have put me there when she got up – and nobody was around.

'Hello?' I meowed as I stood up and stretched myself. 'Where are you all?'

No response. I wandered out of the lounge and upstairs, but both bedrooms were empty too. There was a funny kind of cot that looked more like a cage next to the bed in the bigger bedroom, but Jessica wasn't in it. Nobody was in the little bathroom either and I finally realised they'd all actually *gone out and left me*! I meowed with indignation. I mean to say, I'm obviously used to being on my own at home, quite often all day. But to be left in this strange place, with a huge sea probably on the point of breaking through the windows, and marauding local cats plotting to surround the property – this was a different matter! I trotted around the cottage for a while, crying to myself in frustration, not daring to look outside, and then, suddenly, to my relief, I heard the front door opening and the sounds of my family returning. I was even pleased to hear baby Jessica's shrieking as they pushed her pram into the porch. At least it meant I wasn't alone in this place anymore.

'Make sure the front door is closed behind us before you open the inside one!' Julian was saying.

'There's not enough room for us all in this silly little porch,' Caroline retorted. 'Can't you leave the pram outside?'

'No, we can't,' Laura said. 'I don't want it getting wet if it rains, or damp from the sea spray overnight.'

'No, of course not,' Caroline muttered, her tone of voice a bit odd. 'Can't have Jessica getting damp.'

'I told you this was a bad idea,' Julian said crossly. I walked up to the glass door that separated the porch from the lounge and stared at them through the glass. They were all trying to cram into that tiny space, elbowing each other and almost falling on top of Jessica's pram. What on earth were they playing at? 'I told you we should have shut Charlie in the kitchen. That's what we'll have to do in future, so we can open the doors without having to worry about him getting out. This is ridiculous.'

'I don't think he *wants* to get out, Daddy. Look, he's just sitting there watching us,' Caroline said, squashing herself against the other side of the glass door as Julian struggled to close the outside one.

'We don't want to take that chance, do we?' Laura pointed out.

'But it was really hot in the kitchen! Poor Charlie will be *boiled* in there, without any windows open!'

Boiled? I didn't like the sound of that! Just another worry to add to the list, although personally, I couldn't think of anything nicer than being really hot.

Finally, the outside door was closed and Caroline opened the glass one, almost falling in on top of me.

'Well, we're certainly not doing *that* again,' Laura said as she wheeled the little pram inside, and even Caroline didn't argue this time.

'We went for a walk along the seafront, Charlie!' she said, throwing herself down on the floor next to me. 'There's a really nice beach. We're going down there tomorrow. Daddy said it was too late today – for some reason,' she added quietly, pushing her eyebrows up to the top of her head.

'You know why, Caroline,' Julian said sharply. 'We need to settle Jessica down for the night. It'll probably take a while, being in the travel cot and in a strange place.'

'Yes, so everyone else has to suffer,' she muttered.

'Caroline,' Laura said in a warning voice. 'Don't start. It's been a long day, we're all tired, and—'

'No we're not! *I'm* not! It's not even late! I'd have liked to have a walk on the beach, and a paddle in the sea, but no, we have to come back because of *Jessica*. Jessica needs her sleep, Jessica needs her nappy changed, Jessica needs everyone running around after her like she's the one in charge of this family!'

'That's enough,' Julian said. But he said it in a quiet, sad voice instead of a cross one, and when I looked up at Caroline I saw a little drip of a tear running down her cheek. I rubbed my head against her legs and she curled around me where she sat on the floor, hiding her face against my fur.

'*I* still love you,' I purred at her.

I'd have liked to ask her a few questions, like: What is a beach? What is a paddle? How can you walk on the seafront, if the sea is moving water? And: How did you stop the sea from getting at you? Wasn't it dangerous? But even if I could have got her to understand me, now didn't seem like a good time to try.

Laura carried Jessica upstairs and shut the door of their bedroom, and Julian went into the kitchen to make coffee. Then he turned the TV back on and sat in silence with Caroline, watching pictures of water on it. The water looked very deep and dark, almost worse than the sea outside our window. And then, suddenly, lots of little fish swam into the picture. That was a lot more interesting. I jumped off Caroline's lap and strolled a little closer to the TV. I knew the fish were just pictures – not that I could see the point of it, the whole TV thing is too weird to take on board, if you ask me. But still, they were a definite attraction. I jumped onto the shelf where the TV sat, and put a paw out to the screen, patting a nice bright orange fish that looked like it ought to be tasty. Of course, it just felt hard and cold. But I liked watching the fish anyway, so I stayed on the shelf, aiming my paw out every now and then, to pretend to myself that I was trying to catch them.

Caroline was laughing at me. At least she'd cheered up a bit. Even Julian chuckled as he said, 'Charlie, they're not real! You silly little cat.'

'I know! I'm just playing!' I retorted, somewhat offended. I had a swipe at another, bigger one.

'That's a catfish!' Caroline said, laughing again.

It didn't look anything like a cat to me. Ridiculous name for a fish. But it was nice to hear her laugh, so I had another swipe – unfortunately, just as Laura came back into the lounge.

'Charlie, get down from there!' she said. 'Julian, don't let him do that. He'll scratch the TV. It's not ours, you know.'

I jumped down, chastised again, and slunk under Caroline's legs, but not before I'd caught sight of her face. She wasn't laughing anymore; she was scowling. And even Julian's mouth was turned down at the corners. I wondered if this was how a holiday was supposed to be – everyone snapping at each other and being moody. If so, I was tempted to agree with Caroline that it wasn't going to be much fun, and perhaps we should have stayed at home.

CHAPTER
FOUR

When I woke up the next morning, it took me a while to remember where I was. The sun was shining brightly through the little kitchen window and it was hot in there already. I could hear footsteps upstairs – the floor creaked when anyone walked on it – and Jessica was complaining as usual. I wondered what her problem was. She had an easy life, if you asked me. If she'd been a cat kitten, she'd have been weaned, toilet trained and be learning to hunt by now, but it seems human kittens need babying forever. I got up and had a good stretch. I was hungry, and as nobody had come downstairs yet I had to yowl at the top of my voice to get their attention. Caroline came bounding down from her bedroom, still in her pyjamas.

'Charlie needs feeding, Dad! Shall I give him his breakfast?'

'Yes please, Caroline,' Julian called back. 'We'll be down in a minute.'

'We're going to the beach today, Charlie,' she told me as she dished up my food. She gave my head a little stroke as she put down my bowl. 'Daddy and Laura have promised. I hope you'll be all right here on your own.'

I couldn't stop eating to reply to her, and in any case what was I supposed to say? Now I was getting used to the cottage, I wouldn't have minded being left alone so much if I'd had the run of the place. I'd be out in that garden for a start, sniffing out all the best places in the flowerbeds for my toilet, investigating any smells of mice, voles, rabbits and – always to be avoided of course – foxes. Chasing birds, climbing trees, playing in the bushes, to say nothing of facing any possible opposition from local cats, while I was establishing my position as territory holder. But no, I was apparently going to be a prisoner in this kitchen all day with just a litter tray for company. The only good thing about it was the fact that I couldn't see the monstrous sea from in here. I was pleasantly surprised to find that we'd all survived the night without it getting into the cottage but from what I'd seen yesterday, it was unlikely to give up trying.

'I'm sorry we can't take you with us, Charlie,' Caroline was saying as she poured herself a glass of milk. 'But I don't think you'd like it anyway. And I don't suppose we'll be staying long, because of Jessica *obviously*.'

In that case I was grateful to Jessica for once. I couldn't think what I was going to do all day, apart from sleeping, which I supposed wasn't such a bad idea.

Everyone was soon downstairs having their breakfasts, so after I'd finished eating and washing, I shot upstairs quickly. I had this idea that if I hid under one of the beds, they might not find me when it was time to leave, and wouldn't be able to shut me in the kitchen. The big bedroom was nice and sunny so I trotted in there. There was a lovely clean-sheet smell coming from Jessica's strange new cot. I walked round it, sniffing appreciatively, then jumped up on the big bed next to it and looked down inside. There was a nice fluffy white blanket in there, and a pink toy rabbit with silky ears. It all looked very cosy and tempting. It couldn't hurt for me to have a little lie down in there, could it, while the baby wasn't using it? I jumped down into it from the bed. The sheet was soft, and still warm from Jessica. I purred happily to myself as I started turning round and round to make a nice little nest for myself out of the blanket, finally snuggling down with my nose tucked up under my tail. With a bit of luck, they wouldn't think to look for me in here and I could spend the day in comfort while they were out. I closed my eyes, still purring, and started to drift off into a dream …

'CHARLIE!'

The shriek was so loud and high-pitched, I nearly jumped out of my fur. Laura was standing next to the cot, staring down at me, a look of horror on her face.

'What's the matter? Where is he?' I heard Julian shouting as he came up the stairs.

'In the baby's *cot*, for God's sake! Look at him!' She sounded close to tears. 'You bad boy!' she snapped at me. 'Get out!'

'Sorry,' I meowed, getting up and stretching.

'I said get out!' she said again, reaching down and picking me up quite roughly. 'Take him downstairs and shut him in the kitchen,' she said to Julian, handing me over as if I was something disgusting she couldn't bear the sight of. 'I can't have this, Julian – I'm going to have to strip the cot now and wash everything.'

'Really?' he said. 'But surely—'

'He was curled up on her sheet! In her blanket! With his head on her rabbit! There'll be cat's hairs and … and germs, and goodness knows what … on it all.'

'He's quite clean, Laura,' Julian said gently. He gave me a little stroke as he said it, and I responded with a grateful meow. Of course I was clean! I'd only just washed myself that morning, hadn't I! 'It used to be *you* telling *me* cats were clean animals, remember? When I wouldn't let Oliver get anywhere near Caroline, while she was ill?'

'That was different,' she said, although she didn't explain why. She started taking the sheet and blanket out of the cot, inspecting them as if I might have put muddy paw prints on them.

'Just give them a shake outside,' Julian said. 'It'll only be a few hairs, if anything. He's only been up here a few minutes.'

'They're going in the wash,' she retorted, walking ahead of him out of the room. 'And in future, keep this bedroom door shut, please.'

My world was shrinking. Pretty soon the only place I was going to be allowed to go was my own bed. I could see it coming!

The time passed slowly after they went out. For a while I sat by the washing machine, watching Jessica's sheet, fluffy blanket and pink toy rabbit going round and round, but that quickly got boring. I jumped up onto the windowsill and looked out at the garden. It was frustrating not to be able to tell the birds to clear off. I growled at them from behind the window but I could tell they were laughing at me because I couldn't get out. There was the usual chattering mob of starlings, a pair of nice ripe blackbirds and a fluttering of finches, but every now and then the whole congregation was scattered by a huge ugly intruder who flew in abruptly, landed amongst them and strutted through the crowd as if he owned the place. *Seagulls.* I'd seen them before, of course, flying high in the sky over Little Broomford, wheeling and diving and calling out rudely to each other. Older cats had told me these seagulls were usually making their way to the coast, or sometimes coming inland for a while to take shelter from a storm. But none seemed to live permanently around our parts so I'd never before seen them at such close quarters and, to be honest, the first time one landed in the cottage garden I was glad there *was* a window between us. I'd had no idea they were so big. His feet were huge, and his beak looked like it could swallow a little cat with one bite. I watched him waddle into the crowd of smaller birds, dispersing them just with a glare from his beady eyes, and found myself backing away slightly on my windowsill even though I knew I was safe.

'Don't be such a scaredy-cat, Charlie,' I told myself sternly. 'It's just a bird! Since when have you been frightened of anything with feathers? You've eaten bigger things than him for breakfast!'

That wasn't strictly true. He would've been big enough for breakfast, lunch and dinner for several cats. But I couldn't imagine trying to catch him anyway. His walk was even more ungainly than a stupid fat pigeon's, but when he took off in flight it was with such a sudden ferocious flapping of his huge wings that all the other birds went rushing for cover, and he was instantly airborne, swooping aloft in the currents, calling back mockingly at those who were still on the ground. I've sometimes chased ducks as they take off from beside that big pond in my grounds. They're always good for a laugh. When they take off after swimming on the water, they skim the surface quite gracefully, but on land it's completely different. They have to take such a long, waddling run to get up into the air, it feels like I could bring one down with just a swipe of my paw. But this seagull wasn't like that. There was something arrogant about him that made me quiver from head to tail. I didn't like him. But however much I shouted at him from the window, I had a feeling he'd be back.

I was glad to hear the family coming home at long last. Caroline came straight into the kitchen to see me.

'Have you been lonely, Charlie boy?' she crooned, squatting down to hug me.

'Yes!' I purred into her ear. 'And there was this big seagull in the garden—'

'We had to give up on our picnic and bring it home,' she said, ignoring me. 'The seagulls were dive-bombing us on the beach, trying to steal our sandwiches! Laura was going frantic about Jessica getting her fingers bitten.'

I sat up, instantly alert. So I was right! Seagulls were bullies, aggressive yobs, just as I'd suspected. Trying to steal sandwiches from humans, indeed! Who did they think they were? Next time I saw one in the garden I'd … I'd … well, I'd growl and hiss at him from the window, that was for sure.

'I won't be taking her on that beach again, I can tell you that,' Laura was saying as she came into the kitchen with Jessica in her arms. 'The poor little mite was terrified.'

'*You* were,' Caroline said, half under her breath. 'Jessica didn't even notice.'

'Caroline, put the kettle on, would you, please? And go and brush the sand off your shorts before you sit down in the lounge. I hope you left your shoes in the porch?'

'Yes.' Caroline went to the tap to fill the kettle. 'Just a few stupid seagulls,' she muttered to me. 'You'd have seen them off, Charlie, wouldn't you?'

I was flattered by her confidence in me. But I wasn't so sure she was right.

A little later I was sunning myself on my windowsill, where Caroline had kindly put a cushion for me to sit, when there was a knock on the front door.

'Who on earth can that be?' Laura said. And then, as Julian opened the door, 'Careful, darling, close the porch door first. Charlie hasn't been shut in the kitchen.'

'OK.' I heard Julian respond. And then, 'Oh, hello Mrs Grimshaw.'

'Hello, love,' came a stranger's voice. 'And call me Annie, please. Everyone does.'

I jumped down from my perch and padded into the lounge to investigate.

'So this is your kitty cat you were telling me about,' the woman said as soon as she saw me. 'Hello, little puss. Nice puss!'

I swished my tail at her. For one thing I really object to being called *Puss*. I'm sure you all agree, it's so patronising. If someone wants to say hello to you, why don't they find out your name first? Also, I didn't know yet whether she was friend or foe. She was short and plump, with a red face and a very loud voice that made her sound like she was shouting.

'Charlie. His name's Charlie,' Caroline said, and I blinked my thanks at her.

'Charlie. Right.' The woman nodded. 'Nice markings in his coat, hasn't he?'

'That's because I'm a tabby, you silly female,' I meowed. Didn't she know anything?

'He's a tabby,' Caroline said. 'His father was a tabby, his mother was grey, so some of the kittens were like him and the others were—'

'I see,' the woman said, without waiting for Caroline to finish. 'So, how are you all settling down?'

'Good, thank you, er, Annie,' Julian said. 'The cottage is lovely.'

I could see Caroline was looking as puzzled as I was about this loud voiced, red-faced person who was ignorant about cats. Julian must have noticed because he turned to her now and said, 'Annie owns this cottage, Caroline. She lives next door. I picked up the key from her yesterday when we arrived.'

'Pleased to meet you,' Caroline said politely.

'It *is* lovely here,' Laura agreed. 'Such a beautiful beach. We were surprised it wasn't more crowded.'

Annie's face went even redder.

'Tell me about it!' she boomed. 'We're not getting the usual number of visitors in Mudditon this year. The season looks to be a dead loss. To be fair, it's not been too bad for me, as I get a lot of repeat bookings for the cottage, you see. But the hotels and the bed-and-breakfasts have suffered, and so have all the shops and the cafés.' She shook her head. 'Everyone's having a bad time of it.'

'Why?' Julian said. 'I mean, I know it's a quiet little place but I thought it was usually very popular in the summer.'

'It is, usually. Busting at the seams this time of year, until all this panic about the seagulls.'

I saw Julian and Laura exchange a look.

'We had seagulls coming after our sandwiches on the beach earlier,' Julian said. 'Has it been a problem here, then?'

'I should've warned you,' Annie said, shaking her head. 'You'll be all right if you don't take food down there. They've got so cheeky, you see. Lost their fear of humans, they have. It's because people feed them, if you want my opinion. They should just let them be – they're wild birds, they're supposed to find their own food, but now they've got a taste for ham sandwiches and ice creams.'

'I don't think we'd better go to the beach anymore, then, Julian,' Laura said in a worried voice. 'Not with Jessica being so tiny.'

'But Annie said it's OK if we don't take food down there, Laura,' Caroline said.

'Yes. But of course, even if people are sitting outside the beach café, or in the pub garden, they're getting gulls going after their lunches.' Annie shook her head again. 'It wouldn't have been so bad if it weren't for the media making so much of it.'

'How do you mean?'

'Oh, you know what they're like. The local paper ran a front page story, towards the end of last year's season. *Tourists under siege from aggressive gulls* – with pictures of people cowering on the beach while seagulls swooped all round them. Next thing you know, *South West News* got hold of the story. Then it got into the national papers, and that was when the bookings for this year started dropping off, you see. People were coming out of the woodwork to complain about gulls making off with their doughnuts and biting their babies.'

She stopped, glancing at Laura who was holding Jessica close to her as if she was in imminent danger of attack. 'It was all being exaggerated, out of all proportion,' she went on more quietly. 'You're safe here, honestly, love. Just, well, I wouldn't eat outside, if you're worried, that's all.'

Laura didn't look particularly reassured. 'I take it you didn't hear about this before you decided we were coming here,' she said to Julian in an accusing voice.

'No, of course I didn't. But as Annie says, it's all been exaggerated anyway. Just a few seagulls, for goodness' sake! What else do you expect, in a seaside town?'

'That's what I said,' Caroline muttered, but everyone ignored her.

'Well, it's true the gulls are causing some problems, but it's not as if Mudditon's the only place it's happened,' Annie said. 'And the council's looking into ways of dealing with it. They've put up some notices telling people not to feed the gulls, but it's not enough, in my opinion. They need to do more, or the tourism here is going to go completely down the pan.'

'That's a real shame,' Julian said. 'It's such a nice little place.'

'And people are going to lose their livelihoods, if it goes on.' Annie sighed and looked around at us all. 'Anyway, I just came to check you had everything you need.'

'Yes, it's very comfortable, thank you,' Laura said a bit stiffly.

'Well, look, please don't let this spoil your holiday. As I said, just go inside to eat, to be on the safe side, and you'll be fine.'

'Thank you.' Julian went to the door with her. 'Poor woman's worried about losing bookings herself, I imagine,' he commented after she'd gone.

'She should have told you about it when you booked the cottage!' Laura retorted.

'Come on, I'm sure she's right that it's all been exaggerated.'

'Did it *look* exaggerated when those gulls attacked us on the beach? It was just pure luck Jessica didn't get bitten!'

'Well, now we know, we won't take food to the beach in future. We could go inside the beach café tomorrow and treat ourselves to a nice lunch there. If it stays this hot, we won't want to stay on the beach all day anyway. We don't want Jessica getting too much sun, do we?'

Laura nodded. 'That's true. OK, we'll try the café tomorrow. Or we could come back and eat here, I suppose. I do feel a bit sorry for Charlie being shut up in here all day without any company.'

I meowed with surprise. Somebody was actually considering my feelings! Caroline looked round at me and laughed.

'I think Charlie agrees with that!' she said. And then she looked at her father and added, 'Please can I play games on your tablet, Dad, if we're not going back to the beach?'

'Yes, OK, for a little while,' he said, passing her his computer thing.

'Yes!' she exclaimed happily, jumping up to take it from him. I couldn't understand what the fuss was all about, but she seemed to get an enormous amount of pleasure from pressing that thing and watching pictures moving on it. She sat on the sofa with it and I jumped up onto her lap, purring contentedly. I hoped maybe my little family was starting to settle down now and get along better again. If only it would last!

CHAPTER
FIVE

Are you all keeping up with my story so far? Good. What did you say, Smudge? *When are we getting to the scary bit?* Well, I'm building up the tension, aren't I. Setting the scene. When we do get to the most exciting part, you'll probably be the first one to turn tail and run off in fright!

In any case I was just about to skip forward slightly in the story, because for a while nothing much changed. It was nice sunny weather, and every day they all went off to the beach while I stayed on my own in the kitchen. Sometimes they came back for lunch, sometimes they apparently ate in the café, wherever that was. It was boring. I spent a lot of time asleep. Caroline thought it was boring too, even though she said she liked swimming in the sea. Swimming in the sea? I was quite alarmed for her, as you can probably imagine. We cats have never bothered with all that *swimming* malarkey, have we – what's the point in getting wet all over? It's bad enough if we get caught in the rain, or if we have an unfortunate accident and fall into a pond, which of course is embarrassing as well as being frankly horrible.

The next Sunday – hard to tell what day it was, when nobody had been going to school or work, Julian packed his bag to go off back to Little Broomford. Laura looked sad when they said goodbye, and Caroline pleaded with him to take her back with him.

'Don't be silly,' he said. 'I'll be going to work. You'll have much more fun here, swimming every day.'

But the following day it poured with rain. There was no going to the beach, and Laura was stressed because she'd run out of clean clothes for Jessica, the washer-drier machine in the cottage wasn't very efficient and everything had to be finished off drying inside. I didn't mind, of course, because after all, there's nothing nicer than winding yourself up in clean warm towels and clothes hanging on an airer, is there? I was having a lovely time of it, unfortunately pulling a few things off the airer onto the floor in the process, but when Laura found me she was livid, moaning at me about having to wash things twice, and I ended up being shut in the kitchen again.

Caroline was miserable too.

'I wish I had a tablet or a laptop of my own,' she complained to Laura. 'Now Daddy's taken his with him, I've got nothing whatsoever to do. If you'd even let me have a *phone* it would be better than nothing.'

'You don't need a phone, at your age,' Laura said. 'Why don't you read a book?'

'I *was* reading a book, on Daddy's tablet. I was halfway through it and now he's taken it away. Everyone my age has a tablet of their own. *And* a phone! It's pathetic – I can't even text my friends. I feel like a prisoner.'

But Laura was ignoring her, tutting to herself about the washing. Caroline sat down on the kitchen floor next to my bed and whispered in my ear about how fed up she was. I agreed. Holidays weren't much fun for anybody, as far as I could see.

*

Julian phoned Laura that evening to say he'd got safely home, and then he phoned her every evening after he'd been to work. I heard Laura talking to him, complaining that the weather was awful and Caroline was bored.

'Did you phone for Caroline's blood test results?' she asked the second time he called.

I gathered from her end of the conversation that he had, but that the results still weren't through.

'Oh dear. I expect you're right, it's this uncertainty about her health that's making her so edgy,' she said.

It was true Caroline wasn't being very nice. Every evening she pulled a face when she saw what Laura had cooked her for dinner.

'You never used to be so fussy!' Laura snapped one day. 'I give up! Nothing I cook seems to be good enough for you anymore.'

'I'm not being fussy. I keep telling you, but you won't listen: I just don't want to eat meat anymore.'

'Well, I'm *not* cooking special vegetarian dinners for you, just because you're being difficult.'

Caroline looked like she was going to cry.

'I haven't *asked* you to cook for me, have I? I'll just eat salads.'

Laura gave her a suspicious glance. 'You're not trying to *diet*, are you? Caroline, you don't need to—'

'No, I'm not! I just want to be listened to, and treated like a *person*!' she said, and as usual, ran off to her bedroom.

I didn't really understand. If she wasn't being treated like a person, what did she think – that she was being treated like a cat? It wasn't as if she was being given my cat food, on a dish on the floor, or being shut in the kitchen every time she put a paw wrong. But I loved Caroline best in all the world, so I always ran after her and snuggled up to her when she was upset, anyway.

As well as the phone calls from Julian, I knew Laura had been talking to Nicky. I'd heard her laughing, the way human females only seem to do when they're talking to other females. Towards the end of that first week without Julian, I was lying on the sofa while she was having one of these conversations, and I heard her saying:

'Oh, Nicky, that would be so nice. Yes, please come! It would make it all so much more fun. We can have nice long chats and you can tell me more about what's going on with Daniel. You're right, it might do him good to be left to fend for himself for a week. You will? That's wonderful! Yes, of course Julian will bring you down. And take you back the following weekend. I'm looking forward so much to seeing you!'

Laura was in a much better mood for the rest of the day, and the following evening when Julian arrived back, he had Nicky and baby Benjamin in the car with him. It was nice to see Nicky. She made a fuss of me, and Caroline. Everyone seemed quite cheerful for a change. Laura bustled around turning the sofa in the lounge into a bed, and helping Nicky to put up another of those funny travel cots, for Benjamin.

'You'll have to keep an eye on Charlie,' she warned Nicky. 'He jumped into Jessica's cot last week. We found him curled up in her blanket, would you believe?'

Nicky laughed. 'Ah, how cute!'

'Cute?' Laura repeated, looking startled. Then she sighed. 'Well, OK, perhaps I did overreact a little.'

Yes, you did! I meowed in agreement. At least it didn't seem like Nicky would be shutting me in the kitchen every time I glanced in Benjamin's direction. She was more indulgent to Caroline, too, letting her play games on her phone and shrugging off Laura's complaints about her fussy eating with the advice, 'It's probably just a phase. Try not to stress about it.'

But the happy atmosphere disappeared somewhat during the night-time. One mewing human kitten is bad enough in such a small house. Two is just unbearable. One was waking up the other one, and both of them were waking up everyone else, including me. I burrowed right underneath my furry blanket and put my head under my tail but it still didn't drown out the crying. In the end, I joined in. It seemed like the only option left to me. But that just resulted in Julian coming into the kitchen in his pyjamas to tell me off.

'It's bad enough, without you making matters worse!' he snapped.

I gave up and sat on the windowsill for the rest of the night, staring out at the dark little garden and wishing I could go out hunting.

After they'd all had breakfast, the bad night seemed to be forgotten. The weather had turned sunny again and Julian and Caroline went to the beach on their own, so Laura and Nicky could sit and chat. This seemed to please everyone. I sat on Nicky's lap and purred happily while listening to their conversation.

'Obviously I'm *pleased* his business has taken off so well,' Nicky told Laura, and I quickly realised she was talking about her own male, Daniel. I knew, from hearing them talk so often before, that Daniel had given up his old job in London to start a car repair business. 'And of course I understand that he has to work hard now that he's his own boss. But...'

'But it's not the hours he's working that you're objecting to, is it,' Laura said quietly.

'No. For God's sake, Laura, I'm not being unreasonable, am I? I mean, fair enough if he wants a quick drink sometimes after working so hard all day – I don't blame him for that – but it doesn't stop there. He's in the pub most of the evening, more often than not. It makes me feel like he doesn't even *want* to come home to me.'

'I can imagine.' Laura reached out and took hold of Nicky's paw. 'And he must hardly see Benjamin at all.'

'Some weeks he *doesn't* see him at all. Benny's asleep long before Dan staggers home. And of course, he's often working weekends too. Oh, I don't want to sound like a nagging wife. I know some couples manage without seeing much of each other because of their jobs. But one of the reasons we both changed to working in the village was so that we didn't have to spend all those long hours commuting, and never being at home.'

'And now you must wonder whether you're really any better off.' Laura sighed. 'Well, at least you're happy with what *you're* doing, Nick. The childminding work fits in so well with looking after Benjamin. I'm hoping to find something similar myself, when Jessica's a bit older.'

'You'll have no trouble, with your nursing qualifications. And you're right, I know we women need to find satisfaction with our own lives instead of relying on our men to make us happy. But…'

'You and Dan were *so* happy. And it's not as if you've been married long! He has to be made to see sense.' Laura grinned suddenly and nudged Nicky. 'If he's not careful you'll take off with Kevin the Creep. Then he'll be sorry!'

'Oh, please!' Nicky burst out laughing. 'Don't remind me about Kevin!'

And both of them doubled up with laughter. Nicky was shaking so much I had to jump off her lap. I had no idea who Kevin the Creep was. Where did he creep, and why? Perhaps he had poorly legs. Or perhaps he was a snake, for all I knew. But at least he was responsible for cheering up my two human friends – for now!

Once Julian had gone off back to work again, the atmosphere in the cottage changed. Laura and Nicky were still being happy and chatty together, but Caroline's mood was even worse.

'Now I'm the only one with nobody to talk to,' she complained. 'Even Jessica has got Benjamin to keep her company! Why can't *I* have a friend to stay?'

'Oh, Caroline, be reasonable,' Laura said. 'There isn't room. It's squashed enough here, as it is.'

'Well, after Nicky goes home, then? Please, Laura? If Grace came down we could go out together and I wouldn't be in your way anymore.'

Laura looked shocked. 'You're not in my *way*, Caroline. I've never said that.'

'You don't have to say it,' Caroline grumbled in response. 'It's obvious.'

'That's not true.'

'Isn't it? Nobody cares that I'm totally bored here in this crappy place.'

'Caroline!'

'Well, you think that too, really, don't you? You've only cheered up because Nicky's here. It's totally unfair. I feel more lonely now than I did when I was ill!'

There was a horrible silence. Laura was blinking at Caroline, her paw over her mouth. Nicky, who had left the room while the argument was going on, came back in and put her arm round Laura as Caroline stomped off up the stairs.

'She didn't mean it,' Nicky said quietly.

'Yes I *did*!' Caroline flung back from the top of the stairs. 'You don't understand!'

'We're trying to, Caroline,' Nicky called back. Then, to Laura, she added, 'Why not ask Julian what he thinks of the idea?'

'Seriously? You think I should have *two* moody girls down here while he's at work in London?'

'Actually I suspect Caroline's right about one thing – she'd be a lot happier and less trouble if she had company.'

Laura sighed. 'I suppose so. Perhaps we have been unfair to her. It shook me to the core just now to hear her saying she was lonely. The poor child spent all that time in hospital, and lying at home on her own when she was ill. Have I lost my compassion, Nicky?'

'Of course you haven't. You've got used to her feeling well, now, and she's been trying your patience lately. Plus you've got your hands full with Jessica.'

'I sometimes think Caroline might be jealous of her, you know.'

'She wouldn't be human if she wasn't, a little bit. Especially where Julian's concerned.'

'Yes. After all, it was just him and Caroline, for such a long time. And he was very overprotective about her when she was ill. Understandably.'

'Understandable, yes, but it meant she didn't get to see other children. And now she *has* made friends, she needs to spend time with them. It's only natural.'

'I know. You're right. Well, I'll see what Julian says when we talk tonight.'

I trotted upstairs to jump on Caroline's bed with her. I expected to find her lying flat on her tummy with her face on the pillow, as she normally did after an argument. But to my surprise her bedroom door was closed, and through the door I could hear her talking. I pushed on the door with my head but it wouldn't open, so I sat up and scratched at it with my front paws. The talking stopped. Then she said, more quietly, 'Wait a minute, I can hear someone outside', and came to open the door. She looked down at me and smiled, picking me up and carrying me into the room, closing the door behind her again.

'It's only Charlie,' she said, and I saw that she was talking into a phone. Laura's phone! I meowed with surprise. 'Ssh, Charlie, lie down quietly. It's OK, Grace, I've shut the door again. They can't hear me. So will you come? It'll be so cool. We can go swimming and stuff, and we can sleep in my bed together, it'll be such a laugh! I'm *dying* down here on my own.'

I couldn't hear the other end of the conversation, but Caroline was saying, 'Right,' and 'Yeah, I know,' while she listened, and then she said, 'Yeah, Laura's the same, she just doesn't understand. And everything's about Jessica all the time. It's like I don't matter since she arrived. OK then, ask your mum. And I'll try to talk to my dad tonight.'

After she turned off the phone, she sat on her bed for a while, hugging her knees and humming to herself. She picked me up and rubbed her face against my fur.

'Oh, Charlie,' she whispered in my ear, making it twitch and tremble with her warm breath, 'I *so* hope Grace is allowed to come. We'll have an amazing time together and all the other girls will be well jealous. Surely I deserve this, before they make me say goodbye to all my friends forever and go to that stupid private school.'

And all I could do was purr back at her in agreement. I just wanted her to be happy, you see. How was I to know it was all going to go horribly wrong? Or that I'd end up being responsible for putting everything right again?

CHAPTER
SIX

As it happened, there was another development that evening, which changed everything. I was in the lounge with Laura and Nicky when Julian made his usual phone call. Within minutes of listening to him on her phone, Laura's expression changed and she looked like she was going to burst out mewing.

'Oh, no,' she said, very quietly. 'Oh dear, I was desperately hoping it wouldn't be necessary. Yes, of course you're worried, darling – so am I. Well, the sooner it's done the better. It may still be a false alarm, they just have to check, if there's any doubt, don't they? Right, so you'll take her back with you on Sunday?'

There was a silence as she listened to Julian's response, and then Laura gave a huge sigh and went on: 'She won't want to come back again afterwards, you know. I feel awful now about getting impatient with her. What if her moods and rudeness *are* because she's sick again? She told me today she feels more lonely down here than she did when she was ill. It really brought me up sharply. Yes, she was being stroppy, but even so...' There was another pause, and then: 'Well, she'd started demanding that we let her friend Grace come down to stay for a week – because I've got Nicky here, you know, so I suppose she feels left out.'

It didn't take much guesswork to realise they were talking about Caroline and that there had been some bad news.

They went on talking for a while, with Laura saying 'Yes' and 'I agree', and then finally she said: 'OK then, I think that's a good plan. Shall I call her down so you can talk to her now?'

Caroline came bounding down the stairs as soon as Laura yelled that her dad was on the phone. She looked excited.

'I'm going to ask him if he can bring Grace back with him this weekend,' she said. 'I bet he'll agree.'

'Caroline, Daddy's got something to tell you…' Laura warned her, but the phone had already been taken out of her paw and Caroline was babbling excitedly to Julian about her idea for Grace to visit.

Laura and Nicky exchanged a look, and Nicky grasped Laura's paw. Like me, she must have guessed what the conversation had meant.

'What?' Caroline suddenly demanded. 'I've got to go back to the hospital? Why?' Then she fell silent, the corners of her mouth turning down. 'Oh,' she said quietly. And then: 'Yes. All right. I suppose so. OK. Bye, Dad.'

She handed the phone back to Laura, silently, scowling to herself.

'It's probably nothing to worry about, sweetheart,' Laura began.

'Not for *you*, maybe,' Caroline shot back. 'It's me who's got to go and have the horrible bone marrow thing done again. Why? They said I was better now. It's not fair!'

'No. You're right, it isn't. It's very *un*fair. But we have to trust the doctors. There was apparently something slightly borderline in your blood test, which is why it's taken longer than usual to hear back about it. They need to investigate it further. It might be nothing whatever to do with the leukaemia, but the biopsy is just to rule that out. Did Daddy tell you what he's going to do?'

'Yes, he'll take me back with him on Sunday. That's the only good thing about it. I can get away from this boring dump.'

'You'll have your biopsy done on Monday, and he'll bring you back again.' Laura paused, looking at Caroline's face. 'And if it's OK with her parents, he'll bring Grace back with you.'

'Oh!' She brightened up immediately. 'Really? He didn't say!'

'No, well, he's going to phone her mum and dad now, so he probably didn't want to get your hopes up yet. But, well, I thought it would cheer you up to know that's the plan. We'll keep our fingers crossed, shall we?'

'Yes. Oh, thanks, Laura! It'll be so cool...', and she was off again on a surge of excitement about having Grace to stay. Borrowing Laura's phone, this time with her permission, she ran back upstairs to call her friend again.

Laura glanced at Nicky and shook her head. 'It's as if she's forgotten about the possibility of the leukaemia recurring already! I hope I did the right thing, telling her about Grace.'

'I think so. It'll take her mind off it. I'm sure Sarah and Martin will agree to let her come – especially in the circumstances.'

'Oh, Nicky!' Laura said, wiping her eyes. 'I'm so frightened for her. Please don't let this be bad news. I can't bear to think she'd have to go through all that again.'

'Try to think positive,' Nicky said, putting her arm round Laura. 'At least you won't have too long to wait. Come on, you need to be brave for Caroline now.'

'And more patient with her.'

'No. Then she'll *really* worry that you believe she's ill again!' Nicky said, smiling. 'I think it's important for now that everything stays normal, don't you? She waited a long time to be treated like a normal girl. Don't change that now, unless you have to.'

They hugged each other then, and Laura wiped her eyes again and got up to make a cup of tea. I jumped up on Nicky's lap. I wanted to be hugged too. I was just as worried about Caroline as they were, but I had nobody to talk to about it.

Julian took Nicky and Benjamin home that Sunday when he left with Caroline, who was looking pale and subdued now she knew the hospital appointment was the next day. Laura reminded her, as she kissed her goodbye, that she had Grace's visit to look forward to, and she nodded and gave a little smile. For the next two days until Julian brought her back again with Grace, it was very quiet in the holiday cottage with just me, Laura and Jessica, apart from the times when Jessica was mewing at the top of her lungs, of course. Laura looked sad and worried, and seemed to keep forgetting I was there. I was very pleased to see Julian's car arriving outside again when they came back.

'How did it go?' Laura said, the minute they walked in. I'd been shut in the kitchen, as usual, while the doors were opened and closed but I was listening from behind the kitchen door.

'Fine,' Julian said. 'Caroline was very brave. We just have to wait for the result again now.'

'Well done, Caroline,' Laura said. 'At least it's all over now, and you've got Grace here to take your mind off it.'

'My mind *is* off it,' Caroline said. 'I don't want to think about it ever again. I'm *not* going to be ill again, and I'm *not* going back to that hospital anymore.'

'Well, that's a good attitude to have, but...'

'Let's go and play in my room, Grace!' Caroline said without waiting for Laura to finish. 'Come on, I'll show you round!'

'Where's Charlie?' I heard Grace say. 'Can I say hello to him?'

Oh, at last! Someone remembered I was there! I meowed at her through the door, and then finally I was let out to join in the reunion.

'Come on, Charlie, come upstairs with us!' Caroline said, and all three of us bounded up to her bedroom, the two girls laughing excitedly.

'I'm glad she's OK,' I heard Laura say a bit cautiously as we went.

'Yes,' Julian replied in a similar tone. 'A bit over the top, though, if you know what I mean. All this hysterical excitement. I wonder if she's covering up how she really feels.'

'Scared?'

'Yes. Of course.'

That night Caroline and Grace lay awake for half the night giggling, curled up together in Caroline's bed. Every now and then I'd hear Julian or Laura saying 'Shush! Keep the noise down! Go to sleep!'

Julian went back to work again the next day, and everything settled down a bit, but Caroline and Grace certainly *didn't* keep their noise down. Grace had brought something with her that played music, loudly, and the girls took to singing along at the tops of their voices, sometimes dancing too, and making up their own songs. Sometimes I joined in. I think I sing quite nicely, but for some reason it always made the two girls fall about laughing, which was a bit hurtful.

'Charlie, stop *caterwauling*!' Caroline said on one occasion, making Grace laugh even more. I'd never heard that word before but I guessed it wasn't complimentary. Even Laura was laughing, but then she stopped and, still smiling, said, 'I'm glad you're having fun, girls, but please keep it down a bit when Jessica's asleep.'

When they weren't singing and dancing, the girls were down at the beach. They didn't have to come home for Jessica's feeds or naps anymore, as Laura was happy for them to be out together on their own, as long as they came back at the time she'd told them. One day they were apparently late, though, and got told off.

'You *must* come back on time, or I won't be able to let you go out on your own anymore,' Laura said. 'I'm responsible for Grace's safety while she's here, Caroline, as well as yours.'

'It's just *ten minutes*!' she retorted. 'Chill, Laura, for God's sake!'

Laura sighed. I wondered if she was finding it hard to be *more patient* with Caroline, like she'd said she would.

'Please don't speak to me like that, Caroline. It isn't clever, it's just rude. You can both go upstairs and get changed now – dinner's nearly ready.'

'All right, but I don't want any meat.'

'Well, it's take it or leave it, I'm afraid. I'm not messing around making two different meals.'

The girls went up to their room, and I ran after them.

'See what I mean?' Caroline was muttering to Grace. 'She's, like, *totally* unfair to me.'

'Don't worry, my mum and dad are just the same. They think everything my sister Rose does is amazing, but me, I can't do a thing right these days.'

'But Laura was always really nice to me before Jessica was born.'

'Maybe the younger one is always the favourite,' Grace said.

'That's what I think as well. If she and Daddy were really so worried about the leukaemia, you'd think they'd be nicer to me. It's bad enough they're making me go to a different school from you and all the others! I don't want to go. Sometimes I feel like running away from home.'

'Me too. I don't want you to go to St Margaret's, either. I'm really scared about starting at Great Broomford High without you. But when I try to talk to Mum and Dad about it, they're just, like, *Oh, you'll soon get used to it.* They don't care about my feelings at all.'

'If we ran away together before next week, when we're supposed to be going home, we wouldn't even have to go to high school,' Caroline said quietly. 'And I wouldn't have to go back to that horrible hospital ever again.'

'Unless they found us. Then we'd be in even more trouble.'

'Yeah.'

They sat on the bed together, holding paws, looking so sad I wanted to mew myself. But to be honest, I was too shocked. You can probably imagine how worried I was. Half-grown kittens like Caroline and Grace, talking about running away from home! They'd never survive out there. They weren't used to hunting for their own food, and goodness only knew whose territory they might wander into.

'You mustn't do it!' I meowed at them. 'It doesn't matter if your adults get cross with you – they get cross with me, too, but *I'm* not leaving home, am I?'

Grace finally gave a little giggle. 'We're making Charlie sad too,' she said, jumping up and starting to change out of her sandy clothes. 'Come on, Caro, let's have dinner and then we can write some more songs.'

'OK.' Caroline grinned. 'I'm so glad you're here. Everything feels better now I've got you to talk to.'

But that, of course, was before the Really Bad Thing happened.

*

It was the following day, and as usual the two girls had been to the beach. When they got home it was still warm and sunny, so they went outside to play in the garden. I watched them from my kitchen window as they danced around, shrieking and laughing, pretending to be *pop stars*, whatever they are. It was nice to see them being happy.

'I'm going in to get your iPad,' Caroline yelled, and she burst in through the kitchen door.

I heard her race upstairs to their bedroom, and back down again, turning the music thing on as she went back into the garden.

'You've left the door open,' I meowed to her, but she didn't answer. She was already running across the grass to Grace, the music blaring.

I jumped down from the windowsill and stood in the doorway, watching them.

'You've left the door open!' I called again, but neither of them looked round.

Just then, a stupid pigeon landed on the lawn, right near where they were sitting, and before I even realised what I was doing, I'd shot out of the door and across the grass after him, startling him into taking off again, with a clumsy flapping of his silly wings. Well, it was my job. And very satisfying it was too.

'Charlie!' Caroline screamed, making me jump almost out of my fur. She lunged at me, grabbing me round my tummy so that I wriggled and protested. 'What are you doing out here? Oh, God, I left the door open, Grace! Quick, Charlie, let's get you back inside.'

But needless to say, Laura had already heard the commotion and was coming out of the kitchen door after us, looking cross.

'What on *earth* are you doing?' she said to Caroline. 'He could have run away and got lost!'

'I know!' Caroline said, starting to mew. 'I'm sorry, Laura, I didn't realise I'd left the door open.'

'Well, you *should* have realised! Daddy warned you, Caroline, about keeping Charlie safe. It was you who insisted on bringing him down here with us.'

'I know!' she said again. 'I'll be more careful, I promise. Please don't tell Daddy or he'll take Charlie home and put him in the cattery.'

'Don't say that!' I meowed. I was being carried back into the kitchen now. I must say I'd enjoyed my brief couple of minutes of freedom, though. And I didn't like Caroline getting the blame. I knew I wasn't supposed to go out, after all. It was the stupid pigeon's fault.

'Well, if it happens again, he *will* have to go to the cattery,' Laura said, closing the kitchen door firmly. 'That's if he doesn't end up lost, or run over by a car.'

As you can probably imagine, I had my paws over my ears at this point.

'I said I was sorry!' Caroline mewed. 'I didn't mean it!'

Laura shook her head. 'Go and play upstairs,' she said, as she walked away.

I followed the girls up to their bedroom once again. Caroline was mewing properly now.

'They don't want me around, I'm always getting the blame for everything. I might just as well run away!' she sobbed to Grace.

'If you do, I'll come with you,' Grace said.

'So, shall we actually *do* it, Grace?' They looked at each other for a moment, Caroline still sniffing with tears. 'If we do it now, we won't have to start at our new schools. It's nearly the end of August already.'

'Yeah, let's do it. I don't want to go back home anyway.'

'And I don't want to stay where I'm always getting moaned at. But where can we go?'

'I've got an idea,' Grace said. 'I was thinking about it after we talked yesterday. I've got this great-aunt called Barbara – she's quite old, but she must be nice, 'cos she sends me and Rose money every year for our birthdays and Christmas. She lives in Duncombe. It's the next village along the coast, I saw it when Daddy showed me on the map where Mudditon is. I bet she wouldn't mind letting us stay with her.'

'But your parents will guess that's where we are.'

'No, they won't. The only time they mention her is when she sends us the cheques. We've never been to her house. I've only met her once, as far as I know. She came to stay with us, years ago, but she went home the next day.'

'How would you be able to find her house, then, if you've never been there?'

'It's a really easy address: April Cottage, Duck Pond Lane. I know it off by heart because every birthday and Christmas, Mum makes us write her a thank-you letter for the money.'

81

'*April Cottage, Duck Pond Lane,*' Caroline was repeating. 'It sounds nice. Do you really think she'll let us stay with her? Do you think you should phone her and ask her?'

'I haven't got her phone number. But I'm sure she will. She must really like me, or she wouldn't send me so much money. It was fifty pounds last time!'

'Wow!' Caroline said. 'She must be *well* loaded.'

'Yeah. She's probably, like, one of those old ladies who couldn't have her own children so she loves other people's. I bet *she* won't tell us off all the time.'

'Perhaps she'll adopt us!' Caroline said, giggling.

'Yeah! Then we'll be sisters!'

And the two girls collapsed on the bed together, laughing with excitement. But the whole time they'd been talking, I'd been sitting on the floor listening, frozen to the spot with horror. What *were* they thinking of, plotting to run off on their own like that? They'd get lost! They'd get attacked by feral humans! And their parents would be really, really scared and upset – *especially* as Julian and Laura were already so worried about Caroline being ill again. I meowed at them until I thought I'd lose my voice, but they took absolutely no notice of me – they were too busy giggling over the packing of their little pink rucksacks, putting in pyjamas and socks and a torch and talking about stealing some food and drink from the kitchen when Laura's back was turned.

This was awful. It was as if they thought it was one of those adventure games Caroline played on Julian's computer. I'd heard her shout 'I'm dead! Again!' sometimes when she was playing one of them, laughing as if it was funny to be dead, as if she could come back to life again and no harm would be done. Surely she understood that humans don't have nine lives? If anything happened to her, or Grace, I'd never forgive myself. But what could I do to stop them? I was just a little cat and nobody ever listened to me. I stood for a moment in the doorway of their room, trying to calm myself down. And I made a promise to myself that I'd do everything I possibly could to save the two girls, whatever the danger to me and no matter how many lives I lost in the process.

CHAPTER
SEVEN

I ran downstairs and into the kitchen where Laura was cooking dinner.

'They're talking about running away!' I shouted at her in Cat. 'They're packing their bags!'

'Charlie, please don't get under my feet while I'm cooking,' she said without looking at me.

It's the most frustrating thing, isn't it, when you need to say something really important but you know they won't make any effort to understand you. I meowed my head off at her and tried walking round her legs to get her attention, only to be told off and sent out of the kitchen. I was still hoping there was a chance the girls would realise it was a silly idea and change their minds. But when they sat at the table later, giving each other secret little smiles and eating up all their dinners without making any fuss at all, even remembering to say thank you to Laura for cooking it, I had a horrible, sinking feeling in my tummy that they were purposely being extra good so that she wouldn't suspect anything. They went up to bed earlier than usual – I know, because Laura looked up in surprise and said: 'Well, I might as well have an early night myself, too, while Jessica's settled so nicely.'

The cottage was soon in darkness, and I could hear Laura's steady breathing as I loitered at the bottom of the stairs. I crept up and sat outside the door of Caroline's room. They kept the bedroom doors closed now, to keep me out, but I could hear the girls whispering to each other. Perhaps if I stayed there, I could keep guard over them. I settled down, keeping one eye open, but of course, it's so hard not to fall asleep, isn't it, when it's quiet and dark and you've had a stressful day. Suddenly, though, their bedroom light went on and I heard them padding about, whispering again, and the next thing I knew, the door was opened and they came tiptoeing out, almost falling over me on the dark landing.

'Ssh!' Caroline whispered at me fiercely. Then she picked me up and carried me downstairs with them. What was she doing? Surely she wasn't taking me with them? But downstairs in the lounge, she sat down for a minute with me on her lap.

'I'm going to miss Charlie, though!' she whispered to Grace, and her eyes filled up with tears.

'Don't go, then!' I meowed at her. 'Please! It's a crazy idea!'

'Ssh, Charlie,' Grace warned me. 'Caro, put him down, or he'll wake Laura up. Come on, we ought to get going. Goodbye, Charlie. I'll miss you too.'

They both gave me a stroke, and Caroline's tears dripped on my head. I meowed and Caroline put me down quickly, and before I could even try to trip them up again they were picking up their bags and turning towards the door.

I started to run back up the stairs. If I woke Laura up now, she could still catch them. They'd get a terrible telling off, but it was better than getting lost or attacked, wasn't it?

'Laura!' I meowed at the top of my voice. 'Quick, wake up! It's an emergency! They're running away!'

But her bedroom door was still closed. I started to scratch at it desperately, but then I heard the sound of the porch door being opened. It was too late! They were going! Frantic now, I shot back down again, just in time to wriggle through the glass door to the porch before Caroline closed it. It was so dark, neither of the girls noticed me, and when Caroline opened the outside door I slipped out in front of them and hid, shaking, under the hedge. It was dark, really dark, and the girls were holding hands and shining their little torch in front of them as they walked off. I could see OK, obviously, but I knew their night vision would be rubbish. Humans, as Oliver explained to me when I was a little kitten, are a seriously underdeveloped species compared with us cats. They can't see, smell or even hear half as well as we can, which is probably why they need us to look after them. I only hesitated for a minute, twitching my tail anxiously as I watched their torchlight getting fainter in the distance.

It was no good. I'd never thought of myself as a scaredy-cat, and this was no time to start becoming one. I'd promised myself to do all I could to rescue those two human kittens, hadn't I? So with my little heart pounding in my chest, I set off to follow them into the unknown.

Oh, I'm really sorry, Tabitha. I forgot to warn you, didn't I? Yes, we've got to one of the scary parts now. But look, don't keep mewing about it, you can see I survived, or I wouldn't be here now, talking to you, would I? Is everyone else all right for me to carry on? Any little kittens need taking home? Oliver, can you see if anyone's hiding behind the dustbins? Honestly, sometimes the responsibility of being a famous hero cat is quite a burden.

Well, you can probably imagine how I was feeling at this point in the story. Yes, Tabitha, that's right – scared out of my fur. I was in a strange place a long way from home, with no familiar smells, and to make matters worse, there was a crashing and booming noise going on nearby that I couldn't identify. I scurried along, following the light of Grace's torch and keeping close to the hedges. If circumstances had been different I might have had a sniff around to see what creatures were lurking there, but I knew I mustn't lose sight of the girls.

Then we turned a corner and crossed a road and for a minute I stood rooted to the spot, my back arched, my fur standing on end. I thought we must surely have reached the end of the world. Ahead of us was … nothing. Well, there was *something*, something huge and black that, when the moon kindly poked itself out from behind a cloud for a minute, I could see was moving, sliding backwards and forwards and making the crashing sound I'd heard. It took me a while to realise this was *it* – the sea, that monstrous moving thing I'd glimpsed from the lounge window of the cottage. In the dark and close up, it looked even more threatening. I'd had no idea it was so noisy! *Whoosh, crash. Whoosh, crash. Whoosh, crash.* I wanted to hiss at it to shut up, but I was afraid it would come up onto the road and attack me.

'Let's walk along the beach,' I heard Caroline saying to Grace.

'No! What if we got caught out by the tide?' Their voices carried back to me on the breeze, almost drowned out by the sea's constant shouting.

'OK. But we'd better follow the road along the coast anyway, or we might get lost.'

So we trotted on, with me always at a little distance behind them. For a while the road went along right by the sea, then we turned a corner up a hill and away from it. We went round more bends, down the hill, back up again, and came to a place where the torch showed three different roads.

'I think it must be this way,' Grace said, not actually sounding too sure about it at all, and off we went again.

There didn't seem to be any houses around now. Just darkness and the occasional owl hooting at us from the trees. I was beginning to think I should just run up to the girls and let them see I'd followed them. They'd have to pick me up and take me back to the cottage then, wouldn't they? But supposing they didn't? Supposing they took me with them to run away instead – then I'd be stuck, unable to do anything to help. You might well be wondering what on earth I thought I was going to do to help anyway and, believe me, so was I. I suppose I was hoping I could see where the Great Aunt person's house was, and then find my way back with my amazing sense of smell and memory. I was obviously marking as many spots along the road as I could with my scent, but the occasional whiff of another cat's scent was stressing me out. And I hadn't got as far as working out how, if I did manage to get back, I was going to persuade Laura that I knew where the girls were. There's only room in our heads for one plan at a time, after all.

It all started to go wrong when Grace suddenly stopped walking, saying her shoes were hurting her feet. We'd been walking for ages. If I'd worn shoes on my paws I bet they'd have been hurting too. I don't know why humans seem to need to wear so much stuff on their bodies, but I suppose if we had no fur, like them, we might do the same, especially as we don't like being cold. Once again it seems to be a design fault in their species. I suppose we should feel sorry for them. They look so ridiculous when they take their clothes off, don't they – all bald and bare.

Sorry, I'm getting side-tracked from the story now.

'Well, is it much further?' Caroline was asking Grace as she took off her shoes, rubbed her back paws and put the shoes back on again. 'I thought we might have been there by now.'

'Me too,' Grace admitted. She sounded a bit frightened. 'I didn't think it would be this far, Caro.' There was a long pause. Then she added in a little voice that I could only just hear: 'You don't think we've come the wrong way, do you?'

'Well, I don't know, do I?' Caroline said. 'It's *your* aunt's house we're going to. I thought you knew the way.'

'I thought I did, too. But I'm wondering now if we should have gone the other way along the coast.'

'What? You're joking, aren't you?'

'No. I'm not sure. I told you I've never been there, I just knew it was the next village along, but I can't remember which way. I wish I'd had another look at a map before we started out.'

'So, what are we going to do?' Caroline said, her voice all shaky. 'It's the middle of the night, we don't know where we are, the bags are getting heavy...'

'And my feet hurt. Let's go back, Caro. I'm sorry, it's my fault, maybe this was a bad idea.' Grace sounded like she was going to start mewing.

'I don't know if we'll find our way back, though,' Caroline said. 'We went round so many corners.'

'I'll show you!' I meowed at once. Now was the time to show myself. I'd be their Rescue Cat, leading them home safely ... as long as I could find the right way myself, of course. But before I could run up to them, there was the sound of a car coming along the road behind us. We hadn't seen any cars since leaving the cottage. Probably they were all fast asleep at their homes, and I wasn't sorry, because the road was narrow, with no pavements. You know how aggressive cars can be, wanting the whole road to themselves. This one was purring quite loudly and its eyes were shining very brightly. I jumped back into the bushes, and I saw the girls hiding themselves too. The car roared past us, but as we all stood and watched it continue down the next hill, the light from its big eyes danced off something vast and shiny down in front of us.

'The sea!' Grace shouted. 'We're heading back towards the coast!'

'Yeah, but *which* coast?' Caroline said. 'It could be the other side of England for all we know, the distance we've walked!'

'Or it *could* be the right coast, and we might be just coming into Duncombe. Come on, Caro, let's get going again. It doesn't look far.'

So off we trudged. Before long we could hear the crashing of the sea again, and one or two little cottages loomed up out of the darkness.

'How are we supposed to know whether it's Duncombe or not?' Caroline demanded. She sounded fed up, and I didn't blame her. 'We didn't think this through properly, Grace. It's too dark to see anything, and there's nobody around to ask.'

'And I can't walk any further. I've got blisters on both feet now. We're going to have to stay here till the morning.'

'What?' Caroline shrieked. 'Well, I'm *not* sleeping on the beach.'

'There might be a nice dry bit of sand, up against the sea wall,' Grace said. 'At least it's not cold. What else can we do?'

Shining the torch in front of them, they started to walk down a slope towards the sea.

'No!' I meowed after them in terror. 'The sea will get you!'

But they couldn't hear me because it was crashing so loudly. I have to be honest here. For a minute – just a minute, you understand – I was too scared to follow them. I stood at the top of that slope, looking down at the sea, my tail swishing back and forth for all it was worth. The sea was so big, and I was just one little cat, not much older than little Timmy Kitten over there behind the dustbin. What chance would I have, if it came after me? Then I thought about those two children, all alone in the dark, talking about going to sleep down there. They were braver than me! What a scaredy-cat I was being. But just as I was plucking up my courage to run after them, I heard Caroline calling out:

'Look! The door of this one's not locked.'

I crept a little way down the slope to see what they were looking at. There was a row of funny little houses, each of them looking only big enough for a couple of cats to live in. Caroline had pushed the door of one of them open and they were staring inside.

'There's nothing in here. I don't think anyone can be using it. The others have all got padlocks on.'

'It's not ours, though, Caro. I think beach huts belong to the council, and people just rent them for their holidays.'

'I know, but we need somewhere to sleep, don't we? It's an emergency. Surely it won't hurt. There's nobody around.'

'But what if someone comes and finds us? We'll get into trouble. I'm scared. I wish we hadn't left home now.'

'So do I, Grace, but it's no good us just standing here crying about it. Come on, I think we should stay in the hut, nobody's going to know. If you like, we can take it in turns to stay awake and keep watch.'

'OK,' Grace said, sounding doubtful. 'I do need to take my shoes off for a while. And we could eat some of our biscuits.'

'Yes, good idea, I'm starving.'

And they disappeared inside the little hut together, closing the door after them and leaving me standing there in the moonlight, wondering where *I* was going to sleep. I was starving too, I might add! And tired. It had been a long walk, much longer than my normal evening constitutional round the grounds of my house back in Little Broomford. Thinking about home made me mew to myself sadly for a while. But as Caroline had said, there was no use crying, was there? I didn't want to go too far away from the girls, so I had to ignore the rumbling of my tummy, forget about hunting for food and concentrate on the priority of getting some sleep. I crept cautiously down the rest of the slope and trotted along the path next to the little huts. At the end of the path was a bench, like the ones on our village green where people sit to chat to each other. I crept under the bench and put my head on my paws. I knew I should really keep a watch on the door of the hut where the girls were. I had no idea whether they were in danger or not. But it was no good. Exhaustion overcame me and, before I knew it, I was fast asleep.

CHAPTER
EIGHT

Hello everyone, I'm glad to see you've all come back again today to hear some more of my story. It was a good idea of yours, Oliver, to have a break so that we could all go home for our dinners and get some sleep. I hope none of you had nightmares about my experiences with the sea. It actually doesn't hurt you, you know, as long as you don't walk right up to it. As an experienced traveller now, I can reassure you all of that, but of course, at the time I'm telling you about, I didn't know any more than you do. No, Tabitha, there's no sea around here, I promise you. We'd have heard it by now if there was.

So let's get back to my incredible story, shall we? I was just telling you how I fell asleep under the bench. Well, when I woke up, it was already bright sunshine so I must have slept soundly all night despite the scary situation. I felt bad that I hadn't even managed to keep one eye open in case I was needed to protect the girls. I had a stretch and a quick wash, and padded cautiously along the walkway to the hut where the children had gone to sleep. To my horror, the door was open and neither of them were in there! I looked all around and in the distance I could see another small building, where a female human was carrying chairs and little tables and arranging them outside. And then, to my relief, I saw Caroline and Grace standing in front of the building, taking sandwiches and bottles of water from a young male serving them from the window. It must have been a shop of some kind. I was so hungry I would have liked to run up and grab myself a bite of one of those sandwiches, but I was pretty sure I should stay out of sight. So I slunk carefully along, keeping to the shadows, until I was close enough to hear them.

'Thank you,' Caroline was saying to the boy, giving him some money. 'And we wondered if you could tell us how far it is to Duncombe?'

'We're on our way there, to stay with my aunt,' Grace added.

'Duncombe?' the woman putting out the chairs said, turning round to look at them in surprise. 'You're a bit off the beaten track here, then, my lovely. You need to get back on the main road into Mudditon and it's about five miles further on from there. Your parents waiting for you in the car, are they?'

'No, we're—'

'Yes! Yes, they're ... um ... waiting for us, up the road,' Caroline interrupted Grace quickly.

'Right. Well, that's just as well, because if you were trying to get there without a car, you'd have a job. The morning bus has gone, and the next one isn't till one o'clock. And that only takes you as far as Mudditon.'

'Is it too far to walk to Duncombe?' Grace asked, glancing at Caroline.

'Oh, bless you, you'd take all day and night to walk there, and that's a fact!' the woman said, laughing. 'Get yourselves off back to Mum and Dad now, if they're waiting for you up the top.'

'Oh, it's all right, they're just … um … having their breakfast,' Caroline said.

'Yes,' Grace joined in. 'They said we could come down here and eat ours on the beach.'

The woman stared after them, shaking her head, as they walked away.

'I don't think she suspected anything,' Grace whispered as they passed by without noticing me shrinking back into a gap in the wall.

'Let's sit on the beach to have these, then, while we decide what to do,' Caroline suggested. 'It looks like we'll have to wait for the next bus, Grace.'

'Yes, and then it'll just take us back where we started. I'm sorry, Caro. I *have* brought us in the wrong direction, haven't I?'

'Well, it's not your fault. We'll just have to start again from Mudditon.'

And they proceeded to climb down some steps, taking them even closer to the sea. I must say, the sea didn't look so scary now. It had turned from black to a nice blue colour, with shiny white bits in it, and was swishing backwards and forwards a lot more gently. Instead of roaring and thumping it was just making gentle whooshing noises. I still didn't fancy getting any closer, but it wasn't making my heart race with fear now. I sat down in the shadow of the huts and watched my two bad little human kittens sitting themselves down on the part they called the beach.

Caroline got a jumper out of her rucksack and laid it on the ground, and they spread their sandwiches out on it and started eating. My mouth was watering and my tummy rumbled so loudly I thought they'd hear it. I'd have to hunt soon, or find someone to feed me, or I'd never have the strength to get back home!

At this thought, I mewed sadly to myself with the sudden realisation that I didn't even know when I was ever going to *get* home, if the holiday cottage was even my home now. The girls were talking about getting on a bus! What about me? Could I get on it with them? I knew what a bus was, of course – one comes to Little Broomford a few times every day, as you know. (It's a very large green car, Timmy Kitten, if you've never seen it. It snorts and grunts when it stops outside the village shop, and lots of humans climb onto it with shopping bags.) And of course, the human kittens all get on another bus every day to go to school, don't they. But I'd never heard of a cat getting on a bus, and anyway I didn't want the girls to see me following them. What was I going to do? I doubted I could run fast enough to keep up with the bus. I'd just have to try to find my way back to Mudditon on my own. The girls would carry on trying to get to the place where the Great Aunt lived, risking their lives again with predators and all sorts of unknown dangers, and my mission to save them would have failed miserably. I was despondent now, as you can imagine, as well as feeling hungry and lost.

I wasn't allowed to dwell on this for long, though, because suddenly there was a loud squawking and screeching in the air above me, and out of nowhere, two huge seagulls came flapping down, skimming the roofs of the huts behind me, circling round each other for a minute over the beach and then suddenly swooping down on the two girls, trying to grab their food.

'Leave them alone!' I meowed out loud without stopping to think, but of course, nobody could hear me because of the squawking of the gulls and now, the screams of the girls as they waved their paws around, trying to defend themselves.

'Go away!' Grace was yelling, flapping her paw at one of them. Bits of sandwich fell onto the beach and the gull started grabbing at them with his big hooked beak.

'Ouch! Get off!' Caroline was shouting at the other bird. She dropped the sandwich she'd been holding and jumped up, crying and clutching one paw in the other. 'It bit my finger, Grace! Ouch! Go *away*!' Still holding her sore paw, she started to run away from the gulls, but she was too busy looking back at them and crying, to see where she was going.

'Watch out for the rocks, Caro!' screamed Grace.

Too late. I watched in horror as Caroline's paw caught on a rock and she went crashing down onto the ground. Her head hit another rock and she made a noise that sounded like 'Oomph' before lying very still, with Grace running towards her, screaming her name.

I suppose you all think, if I'm such a brave young cat, why was I still standing up there on the pathway by the beach huts instead of galloping down the beach to help? But look, sometimes things are so bad that even the cleverest cat in the world wouldn't know what to do, right? I admit it, I just stood up there and stared, my heart pounding, my muscles taut and tense, my tail twitching, quivering with fear and indecision. What could *I* do? I wasn't big enough to pick her up, was I? Even *dogs* wouldn't be much better in a situation like this, I'll have you know. They might go and lie down next to the wounded human and lick her face with their slobbery wet tongues, but at the end of the day, what's the point of that? My instinct, to be honest, was to run for my life, but I think it says something for me, at least, that I didn't. I was so scared for Caroline, I had to wait to see if she was all right. The seagulls had no such finer feelings, I can tell you. There they were, squabbling over the last few crusts of the girls' sandwiches, not caring in the least about the trouble they'd caused, and within a few minutes they'd flapped their massive wings and taken off into the sky again.

'Yes, clear off, you bullies, you!' I meowed at them from the safety of the ground. I didn't *think* they'd ever been known to eat cats.

When I looked back at Caroline again, I saw to my relief that she'd now woken up and lifted her head. She let out a moan, and Grace cried out:

'Oh, no! Your head! You're bleeding!'

'Ow, ow, ow!' Caroline was crying, holding her paw up to her head. 'No, it's my finger that's bleeding. That horrible seagull bit me, Grace!'

'*And* you hit your head, look – you've cut it open. Oh, Caro, we need to go to a hospital. I'd better go and get help.'

'No!' Caroline mewed. 'We'll get into terrible trouble, Grace. And I'm *not* going to hospital. I hate hospitals!'

'But you're hurt!'

'I'll be all right. Just give me a minute. I'll ... I'll wrap something round my finger, and maybe you can help me clean up my head ... we can use the sink in that toilet block behind the café.'

She tried to stand up, but she must have been feeling dizzy, like you do if you've chased your tail for ages, because she quickly sat back down again and held her head. There was red blood dripping down the back of her neck onto her T-shirt and even though Grace tried to wrap a tissue round her finger, blood was still coming through that too.

This was no good. I knew I had to do something now, or I'd definitely have to consider myself a champion scaredy-cat for the rest of my nine lives. And there was only one option. I belted back along the pathway to the little café where they'd bought the sandwiches. The woman was inside now – I could hear her talking to the boy, and laughing.

'Quick!' I meowed at them in Cat from the doorway. 'I need your help! It's an emergency!'

'Oh look,' said the boy. 'A nice little tabby cat. I haven't seen him around here before. He doesn't look like one of the ferals.'

'No, he's not. He looks well cared for. Are you lost, puss? He's only a kitten, Robbie.'

She came over and bent down to stroke me. I wanted to tell her I was getting a bit big to be called a kitten, and that my name wasn't *Puss*, but there really wasn't time for any pleasantries.

'Outside!' I meowed. 'On the beach! Quick!' I walked back out of the door, turned round and meowed at them again urgently. 'Come on!'

'What's up with him?' the boy said, without moving.

But the woman, frowning and muttering to herself, wiped her hands on a towel and followed me out of the door.

'What is it, puss?' she said. 'Hungry, I suppose, are you, or…' She stopped, staring down at the beach. 'What's going on down there?' And then she called back through the door to the boy: 'Robbie, call an ambulance. There's been an accident on the beach. A little girl, tell them. Nine-nine-nine, you fool, and hurry up about it!'

Then she ran, as fast as a plump little human female can, down the steps and across the beach, calling out to the girls as I watched her approaching them.

'Don't try to get up, dearie. There's an ambulance on its way.'

'Oh no,' Caroline said. 'Please, we don't need an ambulance. I'm fine. Honestly, we'll just get going.'

'Caro,' Grace said. 'I actually think you should get your head looked at. It looks quite bad.'

'Yes, my lovely, that's a nasty cut on your head, it probably needs stitches – and look at your poor finger too! How did that happen?'

'A seagull bit her,' Grace said.

'Oh, they're a dratted nuisance, those damn birds,' the woman said. 'Now then, why don't you go and fetch your mummy and daddy from the car,' she added to Grace. 'Tell them the ambulance is coming, and I'll stay here with your friend until they get here.'

Even from where I was watching, I could see the look Grace exchanged with Caroline.

'Don't say anything,' Caroline warned her.

'We *have* to,' Grace said. 'It doesn't matter anymore, Caro. It's all gone wrong, and we shouldn't have done it in the first place. We're going to have to go back. After you've been to hospital.'

'Back where, my lovely?' the woman asked, looking from one of them to the other.

Grace looked down at the ground. 'We told you a lie,' she said, so quietly that I had to prick up my ears to hear her. 'Our parents aren't with us. We were trying to run away.'

'But only to Grace's great aunt's house,' Caroline said, as if that made it all right. 'We were going to stay with her.'

'That's why you wanted to go to Duncombe. I did think it strange. And your parents didn't know.'

The girls both shook their heads.

'Are we going to get into really big trouble?' Caroline mumbled.

'Not from me, dearie. It's not for me to say. But your poor parents will be beside themselves, you know. You'll have worried the life out of them. Let me give them a call, for you, shall I? Let them know you're all right?'

'My parents probably don't even know we've gone,' Grace said, starting to cry now. 'I'm supposed to be staying with you in Mudditon, aren't I?'

'Laura might have told them. And she'll definitely have told my dad, and he'll have totally freaked out. He's probably had to come back down from London. I'll be grounded for the rest of the holidays!' Caroline said, joining in with the mewing.

'Well, look, let's not all get ourselves in a state about it,' soothed the plump female. 'First things first, you need that head injury checked, dearie, and here come the paramedics now, so let's get you sorted out and we'll worry about everything else afterwards.'

Two males wearing identical clothing were running down the beach now, carrying bags and looking very serious. They got down on the rocks next to Caroline and started looking at her head and her finger, and talking to her, and to Grace, asking them questions I couldn't hear properly. They took quite a long time. They put white bandages round both her hurt places and, finally, took one of her arms each to sit her up.

'She needs the stretcher,' I heard one of them say as Caroline swayed slightly and put her paws up to her head again. 'All right, sweetheart, we're going to lift you now. One, two, three…' She was laid onto a thing like a sheet that they'd put on the beach. 'Still feeling dizzy?'

'No, I'm all right while I'm lying down,' Caroline said. 'I really don't think I need to go to hospital. I don't like hospitals.'

'It'll be fine, love, they'll take good care of you, you'll see. Anyway we've already told them we're on our way, so it's out of our hands. And now we've got your names and your holiday address, we'll be calling your details over to the hospital so they can get your parents there.'

'But we don't want—' she started.

'Has to be done, sweetheart,' he said firmly. 'No choice in the matter. You'll be glad to see them when they get there, you know. Everyone has arguments, pet, but at the end of the day, they're still your parents, see?'

'I know,' Grace said in a little voice as she followed them up the beach. 'We shouldn't have done it, Caro. We'll just have to take the telling-off.'

I shrunk myself back into the shadows again as they all came back up the steps. I was glad they were going to the hospital. Glad they were going to be taken home, too. But as for me, I had no idea what I was going to do. I followed behind them, at a distance again, up the slope to the road where this big yellow car they called an ambulance was waiting. The female from the café called out goodbye to them.

'You'll be all right now, dearie!' she said.

And then, as Caroline was carried inside the ambulance, with Grace climbing in next to her, the woman said:

'Oh, there's that little tabby cat again! I could swear he was trying to let me know there was an accident on the beach.'

I ran back quickly to the nearest bushes, trying to hide. I'd have liked to get into the ambulance and go with Caroline and Grace, to be honest, but I knew I wouldn't be allowed.

'It looked a bit like Charlie,' I heard Caroline say.

I couldn't help a pitiful little mew escaping from my lips. I felt so lost and lonely now the girls were being taken away. I don't suppose they heard me, from inside the ambulance. But as the men started to close the doors of the ambulance, I saw Caroline's face staring back out at me. I couldn't have been as well hidden as I thought I was. And at the very last moment, just as the doors closed, I thought I saw her eyes growing wide with surprise and her mouth making the word 'Charlie!'

And then they were gone. And I was all alone.

CHAPTER NINE

Despite all my worries, I knew my priority now was, of course, to get hold of some food. I'm not a bad hunter, even though I do say so myself. Oliver here gave me lessons from my early kittenhood. But the scrubby little bush things near the café didn't look very promising in terms of mice or shrews, and the only birds around were seagulls. I certainly wasn't intending to mess with *them* after what I'd just witnessed. I sat down and washed myself again – always a good bet in times of uncertainty – and suddenly a voice behind me said:

'Well, little puss, shall we see if we've got anything nice to reward you with?'

It was the female from the café, and before I knew it she'd picked me up and carried me inside with her.

'What are you rewarding him for?' the boy asked her as, to my delight, she proceeded to pour me out a big dish full of milk and started looking in the fridge for some scraps.

'He came to let me know about that little girl, I'm sure of it. Told me there was an accident down on the beach, he did.'

'Yeah, right, Auntie Stella!' the boy laughed. 'The amazing talking cat, is he?'

'You can laugh,' she said, giving me a stroke as she put down a second bowl, full of bits of lovely leftover fish. 'But

113

I'm telling you, if he *could* speak he would have been saying: *Quick, it's an emergency!'*

Fancy that. At last, a human with a pretty good grasp of Cat! I'd have to converse with her a little more, just as soon as I'd finished this delicious meal. I was enjoying it so much, I was purring out loud while I ate, but I still couldn't help hearing the conversation going on between the female, who seemed to be called Auntie Stella, and the boy.

'Hope the little girl will be all right,' she was saying. 'That was a nasty cut on her head.'

'I thought you said it was her finger?' the boy said.

'I knew you weren't listening. I told you, she hit her head when she fell over. She was running away from the dratted seagulls because one of them bit her finger when it pinched a bit of her sandwich. Damn things are getting to be a real nuisance around here, if you ask me. There've been a few people lately who've been attacked like that on the beach.'

'Poor kid, she must have been frightened. I don't like their big beaks myself.'

'No, well, you're a big wuss, aren't you,' she said, laughing. 'And yes, I do feel sorry for the girl of course, but you know, they were asking for trouble, running away from home like that – silly children. God only knows what might have happened to them, far worse things than a sore finger or even a bumped head.'

I stopped eating for a minute at this, and gave a little meow of agreement. Wasn't this exactly why I'd been so worried about the girls myself? I agreed with Stella – it had been a relief, in a way, that they had to go to hospital rather than carry on with their mad running away idea. But it wasn't until I'd finished my food, licked the bowl clean and started to wash myself that the reality of my situation came flooding back to me in a rush. I was lost and alone in a strange place, and although my poor Caroline was safe now, I had no idea how badly injured she might be or whether the hospital would be able to make her better. Or whether I'd even be able to get back to her again, to find out. Now that my urgent need for food and milk had been satisfied, these worries were suddenly so overwhelming to me that I didn't know what to do, apart from pacing up and down and crying.

'Poor little thing's still hungry,' said the boy, watching me.

'I don't think so, Robbie.' The female bent down and picked me up, giving me a little stroke and looking at me carefully. 'I'm sure he's somebody's missing pet, you know. But he's not wearing a collar.'

No, I wasn't. I never do. I know some of you are happy about wearing them, but personally I can't stand the things. After I chewed my way out of the first two Julian bought me, my family gave up trying.

'Tell you what,' the boy said. 'Shall I put a picture of him on Twitter?'

'Bloody Twitter, leave off about it for God's sake. You're never off your bloomin' phone doing your cheeps and whatnot when you're supposed to be washing up.'

'Tweets, Auntie Stella!' he said, laughing. 'Tweets, not cheeps.' He held his phone up in front of me and pressed something on it. 'Look this way, little cat,' he called. 'That's it.' He pressed again. 'Good one. Right, I'll just share this on Twitter – and on Instagram and WhatsApp, while I'm about it. I'll say he's a lost kitten—'

'I don't know what the hell you're on about, bloomin' *What's Up*,' Stella grumbled. 'How's a picture of him on your phone supposed to help?'

'Oh, Auntie, you're, like, *so* old school,' he said, laughing again. 'The picture goes all over the world! Everyone who sees it can share it with other people and thousands of people will end up looking at him. Someone's bound to recognise him. That's how these things work, see?'

Needless to say, I didn't understand what he meant, any more than Stella seemed to. Caroline had sometimes done that thing before, holding up her dad's or Laura's phone and saying she was taking a picture of me, but when she showed me the picture of a little cat on the phone later, I couldn't understand why she thought it was me. It could have been any little tabby, surely.

'Well, for someone so *old school*, as you put it,' Stella was saying now, 'at least I know the right thing to do with our little furry friend here. I'm going to take him to the vet up the road, and they can scan him with their scanner thing to find out whether he's got an identity chip.'

If the boy responded to this, I wasn't there to hear it. As you can probably imagine, as soon as I heard the word *vet*, I'd yowled in fright and jumped out of Stella's arms. And by the time she'd finished her sentence I was on my way out of the door. Pity. I'd been enjoying her company up till then.

*

I started off running back past the beach huts and past the bench where I'd slept the previous night. Then the pathway ran out, and I plunged into an area of little soft sandy hills with tufts of horrible stiff grass, and spiteful prickly bushes growing on them. It was difficult to run, and I didn't like the feel of the sand – I had to keep stopping and shaking my paws. Yes, it was a bit like when you walk on snow, Smudge, but it was hot instead of cold, and had a gritty feel to it. Sometimes I felt like I was going to sink. But I was too scared to turn back now, in case the Stella woman was coming after me to take me to the vet. It was slow going, and seemed to go on forever. Despite feeling a bit stronger thanks to my delicious meal, I was getting tired from the effort of running on such difficult ground. After a while, I obviously had to stop for a cat nap, so I hid myself behind one of the prickly bushes. I didn't sleep too well – I had a very vivid dream where I was being attacked by a giant dog with big sharp teeth, and I woke up to find I'd inadvertently wriggled closer to the bush and got scratches on my head and my back. Yelping to myself miserably, I trudged on through the sand, without any idea where I was going. It was only by sheer luck that I caught a tiny little bird who'd been feeding from the prickly bushes. I'd never seen one like him before, and he was barely more than a mouthful by the time I'd dispensed with his feathers. But he kept me going for a little longer.

To my relief, soon after I'd finished my makeshift lunch I noticed a rough path leading up the cliff, away from the sea again. Treading gingerly through an overgrowth of the horrible spiky grass, I followed the path and found to my surprise that it came out on a road. Not only that, but I was pretty sure from my superior feline sense of direction that it was the road where the girls and I had started our journey away from Mudditon-on-Sea the previous night. I was heading home, and by following the coast it had taken me far less time than it took us to make the journey on the road! All I had to do was find the little lane that led to the holiday cottage, and I'd be safe, back with Julian and Laura and baby Jessica ... well, eventually Caroline and Grace, too, once they'd been rescued from the hospital place.

Oh, if only that had been true, my friends! I raced along the road and turned hopefully into the next little lane. I didn't recognise it, but I was sure that at any moment I'd smell something familiar, preferably my own scent markings from the night before. No such luck. I went from one lane to another, and then into streets that were more built up, with big houses, shops, and lots of humans wandering about looking in the shop windows. I turned this corner and that corner, but it was no good. I was hopelessly lost.

Finally I turned down a narrow road that arrived back by the sea, but instead of the sandy beach thing I'd come to expect, this time there was just a pathway and a sheer drop down into the water. I backed away from the edge, terrified of falling in, as you can probably imagine, and stared at the sea. It wasn't moving so much here. There were lots of little boats floating on the water – I knew what they were from pictures I'd seen on the television. They seemed to be tied up here to stop them from running away, and they were nudging each other in their sleep, some of them making a jangling noise like the bells on cats' collars but much louder. There were humans around here too, some of them walking along the edge, others sitting on benches looking out to sea. There was a little café, with a picture of ice creams on a sign outside, and a pub – it looked very similar to the one where you live Oliver, in our village – with a roof made of that thatch stuff, and baskets of flowers hanging by the door.

'It's so pretty here, isn't it,' I heard a female human say to her male as they walked past. 'I'm so glad we decided to come to Mudditon again this year.'

So I was right, I thought to myself. *I'm back in Mudditon.* But it seemed Mudditon was quite a big place, even bigger than Little Broomford, and just my luck, I was in the wrong part, with no idea where the *right* part was. There was nothing else for it but to find a warm little spot in the sun behind a wall, and have another little sleep. As always, cat logic decreed that I'd feel better afterwards, and even if I didn't, it'd be easier to cope if I was well rested.

When I woke up, it was dark. I must have had a longer sleep than I intended. For a minute I couldn't think where I was, or what had woken me up. I lifted my head and pricked up my ears. I could hear something, but more to the point, I could *sense* something – some kind of threat nearby. You'll understand what I mean when I say I could feel it in my whiskers. Then the sound came again, and I was up on my paws at once, instantly alert. There was a strange cat somewhere close to me, and whoever it was, he was making the low, rumbling, growly noise in his chest that we all know means only one thing. He wasn't best pleased to see me.

I waited, still and tense, only my eyes moving, checking all directions. I knew I had the disadvantage. I was a stranger, in someone else's territory, and I still couldn't see the other cat. If I ran, I'd only precipitate the attack. But when it came, it still took me by surprise. The skinny black cat jumped out of the shadows and went straight for my throat with his claws, forcing me to the ground.

'OK, OK,' I managed to squawk desperately as I wriggled on my back, trying to get free. 'Sorry. I'll clear off.'

But that didn't seem to be enough for him. With his claws still into me, he rolled us both over so that his back paws were kicking me. At the same time he was trying to get a mouthful of my face to sink his teeth into. Obviously not a happy chap at all.

Now, I should say here that I hadn't forgotten your lessons, Oliver, my mentor. I know you taught me that it's always best to try to resolve a sticky situation like this by the most expedient means possible. By running away. Yes, you did explain that most sensible cats will drop the aggression if you retreat. After all, what's the point in wasting energy? But I don't think this guy had ever had the rules explained to him. He didn't seem to like me at all. I was getting less and less keen on him by the minute, too. Fighting back was now my only option. For a few minutes we rolled over each other, teeth and claws out, screaming abuse at each other. It was the first time ever, you understand, that I'd been involved in a real, full-on, serious cat fight, and looking back I'm quite surprised at how my survival instinct took over. I did get myself free at one point, and managed to jump up on my paws again, arching my back at him, my fur up on end, hissing in his face, swiping at him with my paw. *Take that, you skinny, stinky black Tom cat, you!* And then it happened. Out of nowhere, there was another cat on my back, clawing me, biting me, and then another pounced from the other direction, wrestling me back onto the ground, swiping at my face. I tried to wriggle free but he'd got me in the eye, and I felt it swell up and close. Yet another body landed on top of me and I began to realise I was done for. Oh, I tried my best to fight back, my friends, I can assure you. I didn't want to forfeit one of my lives at such a young age. But it was three cats, or four, or maybe more – I couldn't tell anymore – versus one.

'I submit!' I cried, flattening my ears and trying to roll onto my side to prove it.

The biggest of the cats who'd joined in as reinforcements, a scrawny looking manky tortie with one ear missing and scars on his head, towered over me scornfully.

'All right, boys,' he said to the others, although his Cat accent was so strange, I had trouble understanding him. 'Let's leave the Cowardy Cat to wallow in his own pee, shall we? I don't think we'll see him around here again.'

With that they all slunk away, looking back over their shoulders once or twice to smirk at me.

I lay there for a moment panting, watching them out of my one good eye. I hurt all over, my heart was racing and I felt like crying for my lovely warm bed in my lovely comfortable home with my kind, gentle human companions. But I couldn't. I wouldn't. I was *not* going to lie here and die, and I wasn't going to give those thugs the pleasure of seeing me behave like a terrified new-born kitten. I was *not* a Cowardy Cat! And I was not *wallowing in pee*! The *cheek* of that ugly great bony bruiser – I was a well brought up, decent, family pet who'd been taught to respect other cats' territories and stay out of fights. I wasn't going to stand for this! The physical abuse was bad enough but the insults simply could not be borne.

I struggled to my paws, gasping from the pain in one leg and shuddering at the dark stain of blood I'd left behind me on the ground. I felt a growl growing in the back of my throat as my anger and determination took hold of me. And crazy though it might have been – looking back, I guess it definitely was – I decided that perhaps it would be better, after all, to lose a life defending my honour against that gang of hoodlums, than to lose it lying broken and defeated on the ground. I took a couple of deep breaths – and hobbled after them.

CHAPTER
TEN

Tabitha, please don't cry. Or you, Nancy. I did warn you, didn't I, about the scary parts? Honestly, nobody would believe the pair of you are my sisters, you've got such nervous dispositions, for the siblings of a local hero. Do you want to go home? No? You're too excited about the rest of the story? Well, in that case I'd better get on with it!

Can you imagine how I felt, my friends, limping along the pavement in that strange place, with every bone in my body hurting and blood dripping down my face, knowing I was probably going to be finished off at any moment? If I hadn't been so angry, I'd have gone in the opposite direction, trust me. But I hobbled on, round the corner where I'd seen my attackers go, and into an alleyway that eventually came out in a small yard. There were big tall buildings around the yard, but it didn't look like anyone lived there – everything was closed up and some of the windows were broken. There was one lamppost, right in the far corner and, as I approached, I saw him sitting there – the big one-eared tortie – and he was on his own. I had the advantage of being in the shadows, but on the other hand he was twice my size and presumably had two working eyes against my one.

I flattened myself against the wall of a building and crept slowly closer. He was engrossed in washing himself, and didn't even look up once before I finally made my move. I'd like to say I pounced, but although I'm proud of the fact that I took him by surprise, I have to admit it was more a case of flopping myself at him, with what little strength I had left. I'd timed it so that I got him while he was engaged in cleaning his private parts, so I was able to knock him off balance without too much trouble. He made a grunt of surprise as he toppled backwards, and I immediately threw myself on top of him and, yowling my fury straight in his ear, I took a very satisfying bite out of his neck.

'Ouch! What in the name of bloody catnip?' he squawked, in his peculiar Cat accent. 'Get off me! Who the dog's backside are you? Boys! Where are you! I'm being attacked!'

He squirmed, trying to get to his paws, but I aimed a swipe for his face and followed it up with another bite. Nevertheless, it didn't take long for him to throw me off. He was skinny, but muscular as well as being big, and I hadn't hurt him anywhere near as much as I'd been hurt. I put my head down and hissed, waiting for him to start on me again, but just as he was aiming his claws at me, he suddenly blinked in surprise and growled: 'Well, by my tail and whiskers! If it ain't the little Cowardy Cat, come back for more.'

'Take that back,' I hissed, forcing myself to sound really brave. 'I'm *not* a Cowardy Cat. It was four or five of you against one.' Out of the corner of my good eye, I saw some dark shapes moving towards us in the shadows. 'And if your *boys* are coming back to do the same thing again, then they'll probably succeed in finishing me off. If you think that's a fair fight, then I don't know what kind of hovel you were all brought up in...'

'Talk posh, don't you, Sunshine?' He lowered his paw. 'All right, boys!' he called. 'It's only the little Cowardy—' He stopped, looked me up and down, and then went on: 'The little *brave* tabby from earlier on. No, leave him alone, Black. We've already done him enough damage, and it took a lot of guts for him to come after me. He doesn't look very old but he's a good fighter.'

And do you know what? He lay back down again, deliberately, in the submissive position in front of me. I could hardly believe my one eye. The other cats hung back, waiting, and when he got to his paws again he came up and rubbed himself against me.

'Sorry about earlier,' he said gruffly. 'But for the love of catnip, what's a posh lad like you doing around these parts?'

'I got lost,' I said. Now the danger seemed to be over and I was apparently still alive, I was starting to shake from head to tail. 'My humans are staying somewhere around here, but I don't know where.'

'*Your humans?*' he repeated, looking at me as if I'd spoken in Dog or Cow or something. 'You have your own pet humans?'

I might be a bit slow, but it was actually only then that the truth dawned on me. These guys were the real deal – the *alley* cats we've all been warned to stay away from, the ones our mothers told us scary stories about before we could even walk. *Ferals.* The very word strikes fear into the heart of a cosseted domestic cat. Yes, I'm not surprised you've all frozen in terror.

'Um, yes,' I squawked, starting to back away.

'And is it true that they let you live in their houses?' he asked, staring at me now with wide eyes. 'And feed you, and give you funny names? Don't run away, I'm not going to hurt you anymore. I want to know all about it. Gather round, boys. This young tabby lives with humans! *Have* they given you a funny name? What is it?'

'Charlie,' I meowed quietly. They all stared at me in stunned silence.

'*Charlie*,' the tortie repeated. 'Blimey whiskers. It makes you sound ... like a human.'

'So what's *your* name?' I asked timidly.

'Name?' he retorted. 'We don't have names! Why would *we* want fancy names?'

'So you could call to each other?' I suggested.

'Oh, that! We just call each other what we *are*. Like: *he's* black. *He's* tail-less. And him over there, he's stinky.'

'Oh, I see.' As far as I was concerned, they were all pretty stinky. But I didn't think it'd be wise to mention that, at this point. 'So what are *you*?'

'Big, of course,' he said, stretching himself up to his full height. 'That's why I'm in charge.'

'Right.' And I couldn't help it. Despite everything, I couldn't ignore my upbringing, you see. It was only polite to say, rubbing my face against his: 'Well, I'm pleased to meet you, Big.'

'You too, um, *Charlie*,' he said, seeming to have difficulty with the pronunciation. 'And if you're lost, I suppose you'd better stick with us. At least till you find your pet humans again, eh? You won't last long in this area without us to protect you.'

Well, that'd certainly be an improvement on having them beating the poo out of me.

'Right, OK, thank you. You live around here, do you?' I added, as we didn't appear to be hurrying off home anywhere.

'Born and bred in this yard,' Big said proudly. 'All the boys were. The whole of this area – the yard and the alleyways off it – is our territory. Humans don't like us, of course, apart from the odd one or two who seem to feel sorry for us and bring us food occasionally.'

'So you have to hunt every day, I suppose?' I stared around me. There didn't seem to be any bushes or trees or even grass around. 'Just mice and rats, is it?'

'And fish, if we can get it,' said Black, who'd been creeping closer to get in on the conversation.

'Yeah, the humans go out in their boats every morning and come back with loads of them,' Big explained. 'We take it in turns to creep up and try to nick a fish or two without them seeing us. Most of them shout at us or kick us if they catch us at it, but sometimes there's a tame human who actually *gives* us a fish.'

'Not often, though,' Stinky complained. 'You'd think they'd share, wouldn't you – I can't see why they need so many fish just for themselves.'

'Greedy,' said Big. 'That's their trouble.'

I yawned. It was fascinating, now everyone had calmed down, to hear about the ferals' lifestyle, but I'm sure you'll agree I'd had a tiring day one way or another, and it must have been the middle of the night by now. I looked around me, puzzled.

'Where are your beds?'

'*Beds?*' They all stared at me. 'Are you being funny?'

'No. Sorry, why?'

'We sleep here, in the yard, *Charlie*. In corners, behind walls, in doorways, or down one of the alleyways. Sometimes in summer we sleep on the roof tops,' Big said. 'I'll find you a little place near me, when it's sleep time.'

'Isn't it sleep time yet, then?' I asked, stifling another yawn. I'd always thought any time was sleep time for cats!

'No, it's scavenging time, for catnip's sake,' he said, looking exasperated. 'Don't you know anything?'

Evidently not. I didn't even know what scavenging was, but I wasn't about to admit it.

'It's how we get most of our food nowadays,' Tail-less kindly explained, seeing my blank look. 'Humans make it easy for us, they're so lazy and untidy. They feed in the street, don't finish their food, and throw what's left over in bins. But sometimes they just drop it on the ground instead. And also the bins get full up, and overflow, so there's always plenty for us. The best places are outside their eating houses. *Cafés*, they call them,' he added, as if I didn't know. 'And the ones they call *fish and chip shops* – they're the best. And *takeaways*.'

The others were all meowing agreement.

'Come on, then, let's go,' Stinky urged. 'I'm starving.'

So was I, now he came to mention it.

'You'd better come with us,' said Big. 'Seems like you need an education.'

And with that, he led the way back out of the yard. I watched them moving off for a minute. I was so tired, and so sore from my wounds, that getting an education wasn't exactly uppermost in my mind. But what else could I do? As he'd pointed out, it seemed I'd be in danger around here if I didn't stick with them.

'Why can't we go in the morning?' I called out, in one last attempt to get time for a nap.

They all turned round and stared at me again. I was getting used to it.

'In the *morning*?' squawked Black. 'Don't be ridiculous!'

'We can't scavenge humans' waste food during the daytime,' Big explained patiently, as if I was a particularly dim little kitten. 'That's when the seagulls are out in force.'

'Oh. Yes, I've seen some of them around. They're not very nice, are they?'

'*Not very nice!*' Tail-less mimicked. 'What an understatement, eh, boys? They're thieving, spiteful, vicious hoodlums, that's what they are,' he added in a hiss. 'We hate them, and they hate us. They've been known to kill cats, you know.'

That's rich coming from you lot! I wanted to meow, knowing how close they'd come to killing this particular cat themselves. But I thought better of it, since I'd apparently now been adopted as their slightly odd posh friend.

'I can well believe it,' I said instead, limping after them. 'One of them bit my human kitten's finger.'

'It probably deserved it,' Big said dismissively. 'But that's not the point. We don't go anywhere near the bins when they're awake, right? We wait till the eating houses are closed for the night, then we go and get as many scraps as we can before the gulls wake up.'

'It's bad enough risking life and paw when the fishing boats come in,' Stinky told me. 'The gulls follow the boats back in from the sea – loads of them, all swarming together and shouting their heads off. If we want to try sneaking a fish when they're unloaded, we have to be very quick and very crafty.'

'One of us makes a run for the fish, while the others watch out for gulls and try to protect him,' Big explained.

It sounded so dangerous, I wondered why they bothered, instead of just hunting for easy prey like mice. But then I remembered how delicious a mouthful of lovely fresh fish tasted, and my mouth started to water. I was weak with hunger. I'd have to take my lessons from these boys, whether I liked it or not.

By now we were approaching the area where all the shops were. I stayed close to the ferals, unsure what the proce-dure was.

'Stay in that doorway, and watch me,' Big said.

He stalked towards a rubbish bin outside the shop next to the one where I was waiting, and with a quick glance around him, leapt up onto the top of the bin, grabbed something in his mouth and ran back to me. It was all done in the flash of a cat's eye.

'Here you go,' he said, dropping his trophy at my paws. 'Help yourself. I'm going back for more.'

I sniffed the lump of food. Fish! Yes – just what I needed. I took a hungry bite and my appetite diminished straight away. What kind of fish was this? The outside was hard and crunchy! I spat it out, and tore at what was left of it with my teeth to investigate further. The inside looked nice enough – good white fish meat, a bit bland, but I had to be grateful for small mercies.

'What on earth is it?' I asked Big when he returned with another lump from the bin. 'It's all crunchy and horrible on the outside!'

'Bit ungrateful, aren't you?' he remarked. 'Is it true what they say about domestic cats – you're so pampered, you can afford to be fussy eaters?'

'Sorry,' I said, immediately feeling ashamed. 'You're right. I've been used to the lovely food my humans hunt for me in the supermarkets. I suppose I *am* spoilt.'

'Don't worry about it,' he said easily. 'You'll have to eat whatever you can get now, like us, or you'll starve. This is the type of fish humans buy from fish and chip shops. For some reason they like it covered in this stuff. Batter, they call it. Ruins the taste, doesn't it, but the fish meat inside is OK, until it starts to go off, anyway. That's why we only take what's at the top of the bin.' He took a bite of the second lump of food he'd brought back. 'Want to try some of this?'

'What is it?' I asked doubtfully. It looked like mouse meat wrapped in bread.

'They call it a burger. Don't your humans eat them? I thought they all did. Round here, they even walk along the street eating them. Crazy! Then they wonder why the seagulls attack them!'

'I think they do have them at home sometimes,' I said. Just thinking about Laura cooking the dinners for my family made me feel sad all over again. 'But I've never tried one.'

'Help yourself. I'll see what else I can find. Then we'll move on to catch the others up at the Chinese takeaway. That'll be an experience for you!'

I nibbled at the burger, discarding the bread, and then felt bad for being fussy. The meat part wasn't bad, but it was smothered in something yellow and spicy that made me want to throw up. Then Big came back again, this time with a mouthful of chips. I knew all about *them* – I'd occasionally stolen one or two from my humans' dinner plates when they hadn't eaten them all. But these were different: greasy and slimy. I forced one down and hoped I wasn't going to have an upset stomach.

'If this is the sort of food humans eat around here,' I commented, 'they must have very strange tastes.'

'Well, let's face it,' he said. 'Humans are just plain weird. I've given up trying to work them out. I can't understand what you see in them.'

And so the night went on. Exhausted, aching and starting to feel sick, I was forced to sample things I thought no self-respecting cat would ever let pass their whiskers. Now that my hunger had been eased, I really didn't *want* to try balls of pig meat smeared with a bright red spicy sauce, or prawns that had been ruined by being covered in that awful batter stuff. But I didn't want to offend Big and his friends, who were teaching me how to scavenge and might just as happily have left me to starve.

'You'll get a taste for these things in due course,' Tailless tried to comfort me as I retched on a piece of funny-tasting red sausage wrapped in stale bread.

But I wasn't sure I ever could. When they finally led me back to their yard, Big showed me his sleeping place in a mossy crevice of a brick wall – and taking pity on me, offered to share it with me. Then I lay awake for ages, watching the dawn break, thinking about Julian and Laura, and whether they'd gone to the hospital to find Caroline and Grace. And whether Caroline's wounds hurt as much as mine did. And ... whether they all missed me. But eventually I mewed myself quietly to sleep, curled up against Big's bony back, and dreamt I was back here in Little Broomford, chasing stupid pigeons in the Big House grounds. Oh, if only that dream would come true!

CHAPTER
ELEVEN

When I woke up the sun was shining brightly, but I could see from the length of the shadows that the day was already half over. I guessed I'd have to get used to this more nocturnal lifestyle while I was living with the feral gang. I just hoped it wasn't going to go on for too long.

'I need to start exploring the town again, to try to find my human family,' I told Big when I found him washing himself under the lamppost. 'It's not that I don't appreciate your generosity in letting me stay with you and the boys. It's very good of you to give me your protection.'

As you can tell, despite him calling me a hero the previous day, and seeming to like me well enough now, I was still a little wary of Big and I didn't want to offend him.

'All right, all right, no need for all that,' he said. 'I get it, you're not one of us, and I suppose you're missing your nice easy life with your tame humans.' He paused. 'But I'm not sure you should be off exploring on your own. You're only a kid, and not very streetwise. You'll probably get yourself lost again. Your eye is so swollen you can't see properly.'

Yes, and whose fault was that?

'What am I going to do, then? If I don't find them soon, they might finish their holiday and go back to our normal home. And I'd never be able to get back *there* on my own. It's on the other side of the universe – our car had to carry us here and it took nearly a whole day.'

'Oh, they're *holiday* humans, are they? Huh! They're the worst sort,' he said.

'Mine aren't!' I retorted. 'They're very kind humans, actually, and they love cats.'

'I bet they wouldn't love *us*. Humans never do. They treat us like we're rats,' he said. 'But still, I think a couple of us should come with you if you're going to start touring the streets looking for them. I warn you, though, there could be a few fights if we trespass into other cats' territories.'

'I expect you'll win, though.'

'Of course we will. That goes without saying!'

Black, Stinky and Tail-less had joined us by now, and Tail-less was meowing about going to the harbour to try to steal a fish or two.

'Good idea,' Big agreed. 'Let's show our new little friend how it's done. We have to be careful, as well as crafty,' he said, as we began to move off.

'Yes, you explained about the angry humans and the vicious seagulls,' I said. It didn't sound like my idea of fun. 'Shouldn't we just stay away?' I think I'd proved myself not to be a Cowardy Cat now, but to be fair, my bites and scratches from the previous day were still sore, and I was walking with a limp.

'What, and miss the chance of a nice bit of fish, fresh from the sea?' squawked Stinky.

'You can stay in the shadow of the humans' pub place, and watch us from there,' Big said. 'Tail-less will stay with you and watch out for seagulls swooping down. Black and Stinky – you stand guard by the harbourmaster's hut as usual. I'll be the runner today. If anyone sees one of those humans by the boats, coming after me, you give me the cat-call, OK?'

Despite my anxiety, the whole operation was actually carried out so quickly, the humans still had their backs turned when Big returned, a whole fish hanging from his mouth.

'Tuck in,' he meowed to me and Tail-less. 'I'm going back for another.'

'Cod. Yum, my favourite,' said Tail-less.

And I have to admit, it was the freshest, most delicious fish I'd ever tasted. No wonder these boys took such a risk for it.

Suddenly, there was a loud yowl of warning from where Black and Stinky were positioned. Big, another fish in his mouth, turned tail and dashed back towards us. The two humans had turned away from their boats and one of them was throwing something at him while the other one yelled:

'Bloody cats! Thieving bloody varmints! Get out of here, you pesky moth-eaten bag of bones!'

'Phew!' meowed Big as he skidded to a halt beside us. 'That was a close shave.'

'I can't believe how rude that human was to you,' I sympathised. 'There was no need to call you names like that.'

Big and Tail-less both gave me a funny look.

'Oh, he was just making a lot of angry growling noises,' he said without much interest.

I thought perhaps he'd been running too fast to hear what was being said. But a little later, while we were finishing off the fish round the back of the pub, a couple of humans strolled past, holding each other's paws, the way they do sometimes if they like each other.

'Ah, look at the poor little cats,' the female said, stopping and bending down towards us. 'Do you think they're strays, Kev?'

'No, I think they're feral cats, Gemma. Don't touch them, they might be carrying some kind of disease. And they might attack you.'

'What a cheek!' I muttered to Big, but he wasn't taking any notice.

'Poor things,' said the female. 'It's not their fault, Kev – they were probably someone's pets once. They might have got lost, and turned feral to survive.'

I pricked up my ears at this. Was I going to *turn feral* too, if I didn't find my way home? Would I end up living my whole life like this, stealing fish, raiding bins for humans' rubbish, sleeping rough and starting to talk in the strange, guttural Cat accent of my new friends? I started to shiver at the thought of it.

'No, most of them will have been born in the alleyways around here to feral mothers,' said the male. 'They're vermin, Gemma. There's a lot to be said for the idea of a cull.'

'What?' She let go of his paw, looking at him in horror. 'I can't believe you just said that! What have these poor little things done to deserve that?'

As you can imagine, I was liking her a whole lot more than her male! I couldn't help myself from purring and going to rub myself against her legs in gratitude. It seemed ages since I'd had any human affection.

'Don't let it touch you!' the male said, pulling her away from me. 'It's probably riddled with fleas and disease.'

'I'm not!' I meowed. 'I'm a pet! I'm lost! I want some love!'

'What are you doing?' Big meowed at me at the same time. 'Stay away from them, Charlie, for the love of catnip! You don't know whether they're tame humans or not.'

'They were. Well, *she* was,' I mewed sadly as I watched them walk away. I noticed they weren't holding paws anymore and the female was walking apart from the male, looking cross. 'She was being kind, but the male was horrible, wasn't he.'

All the other cats were staring at me.

'So what are you, some kind of expert in human behaviour now?' Big demanded. 'I'm telling you, it's impossible to know what they're thinking. Not all of them are like the pet humans you used to have, you know.'

The words *used to have* filled my heart with despair. I *was* going to go back to my family. I had to find my way back! But in the meantime, something was puzzling me.

'Didn't you hear what that male was saying?' I asked Big quietly. Maybe he was a bit deaf.

'I didn't notice any particular body language from him, no,' he said. 'But then again, humans don't use much, do they.'

143

'I mean what he was *saying*. Verbalising.'

'Oh, you mean all that growling and whining they do. It's meaningless. Don't worry about it. It's only when they bark like dogs we have to make ourselves scarce.'

'No,' I protested, 'it's not meaningless at all. Do you mean to say you can't understand Human?'

'There's nothing to understand,' he insisted. But he was giving me another funny look now. 'You're not telling me you think you can translate it?'

'I thought all cats could. We're born bilingual. I mean, we can't *speak* it, of course, and they can't understand Cat, sadly, but...'

Stinky and Black were sniggering. Big and Tail-less were frozen on the spot, looking at me as if I had two heads.

'Prove it,' Tail-less demanded.

'Yeah, go on,' Black said. 'Tell us what those humans were saying.'

'All right. But you won't like it. The male said we were all vermin, we carry disease, and we should be culled.'

'What?' Stinky squawked. 'I hope you're making this up!'

'No, I'm not. But the female felt sorry for us and told him off.'

There was silence for a while. They were starting to look at me differently – almost like they respected me.

'And you're saying you can understand *everything* humans say?' Big demanded.

'Well, they do sometimes come out with new words I haven't heard before. But I can usually get the gist of it.'

'I suppose it's because you were born to domestic cat parents,' he said wonderingly, 'and you've been raised by humans, lived with them from kittenhood.'

'Well, all the cats I know can understand Human,' I said. 'So I didn't think it was unusual.'

'We've only ever had other feral cats for company,' Stinky said. 'All of our mothers were ferals. All the females we mate with, and all our kittens, are ferals too.'

'Yeah, we've never been friends with a posh domestic cat like you before,' Black said. 'We normally leave them for dead if they stray into our territory.'

'I know.'

There was another silence.

'Well, we're sorry about that now, aren't we, boys,' Big said. 'And it looks like you might be a useful little cat to have around, after all.'

'How?'

'You can give us the low-down on what any passing humans are saying. There are always rumours going around our community about them plotting to poison us or chase us out of town, but we've never known whether there's any truth in it all.'

'Good idea,' Tail-less said, 'And in return we'll keep trying to help you find your humans. You don't belong round here, that's for sure. You're ... well, you're *different*.'

I wasn't sure if the look he was giving me now was one of admiration or wariness. But it was a fair enough bargain. And if it resulted in me finding my family, preferably before I turned feral myself, it was the only way to go.

'OK,' I said. 'I'll be your translator. Now, can we start searching for my holiday home?'

That evening, while Black and Stinky went scavenging for scraps in the bins as usual, Big and Tail-less took me on a tour of some of the streets of the town. The houses here seemed mostly to be very large, with signs outside printed with names in Human.

'Hotels,' Big explained. 'Holiday humans stay in them and get fed. The bins round the backs are good for scavenging. I'm guessing your humans will be in one of these?'

'No,' I meowed sadly. 'They're staying in a little house – a cottage. It's in a quiet lane, not a street like this with pavements. It's near the sea.'

'Hmm. Sounds like it's further out of town. Well, we've covered quite a lot of ground already tonight. I suggest we call off the search for now and get something to eat. Don't worry, young Charlie.' He was sounding quite affectionate towards me now. 'We'll search the streets every day. We'll get there in the end.'

I hoped he was right. But I was beginning to feel like it might be an impossible mission.

CHAPTER
TWELVE

Yes, my friends, you're right in thinking I was becoming used to the feral cats by now. After living with them like that, I can tell you I actually have a lot of sympathy for them. They've got a terrible reputation, and it's true they can be very aggressive. I've got the scars to prove it! But it's understandable. They've got tough lives, and after all, they didn't choose to be born into those circumstances. I understand now why they hang around in gangs, too. On their own, they'd be prey to all sorts of dangers. They need each other for protection. It's all very well for domestic cats like us to say we enjoy our own company. We can pick and choose which cats we want to spend time with, and who's allowed into our territory, or we can be completely solitary if we want to. We've got humans to protect us and we can choose to stay inside our nice warm homes whenever we like. I found myself wishing I could do more to help those cats, but to be honest, I don't think they'd have been able to adapt to a life like ours.

For one thing, none of them had ever heard about going to the vet for *that operation*. They looked absolutely horrified when I told them I'd had it.

'I thought you said your humans were kind!' Black said.

'They are. I know it seems like a cruel thing to do, but honestly, it's just like my friend Oliver explained to me when I was a little kitten: what you've never had, you never miss.'

'Well, I'm as sure as a dog's backside that *I'd* miss it,' Big said. 'We all would! Apart from the fresh fish, it's the only thing that makes our lives worth living.'

I thought about this for a while. There were so many things that made *my* life worth living when I was at home in Little Broomford, I felt almost guilty about it, not to say even more homesick.

'We have humans to love us,' I tried to explain. 'We sit on their laps and get stroked and cuddled. It makes up for not mating.'

'You must be joking,' Stinky said. 'That sounds awful. I'm surprised you put up with it.'

'And it can't possibly compare with a quick session with Blotchy Face when she's on heat,' Black put in.

'Yeah, she'd soon make you forget about your humans, Charlie!' said Tail-less.

I felt sorry for Blotchy Face, whoever she was. She must have spent her whole life being pregnant and having loads of kittens.

As the boys continued to discuss their mating rituals, I distanced myself from the conversation. I couldn't help thinking about my sisters back at home. I was glad to remember most of you females have been spayed.

'I was neutered before I was old enough to want to mate with anyone,' I tried to explain to the boys when their banter had finally died down. 'Our humans get us done because they want to take care of us. They don't want our females to have lots of kittens who might not be looked after by anyone.'

'Our females look after their own kittens,' Black retorted. 'Well, for a few weeks, anyway, till they can fend for themselves.'

And then they just end up living rough, like you, I wanted to say. But I knew it was no use. They'd never understand. The gulf between our lifestyles was too vast.

But the one thing they envied, once they were actually convinced I wasn't faking, was my ability to understand Human. That same day, I proved my worth to them by translating a very interesting conversation that was going on outside the little café near our yard. Two females were sitting together at a table with cups in their paws, talking earnestly about seagulls.

'Damn things are a real nuisance,' one of them said, pointing out a couple of gulls circling above. 'Ever since a few people were attacked, it's been putting off holiday-makers from coming here.'

'I know. Business is going down the pan for the beach cafés and kiosks. Nobody wants to risk eating in the open air.'

I remembered how we were told the same thing by the Annie female who owned our holiday cottage. And because I still felt cross about Caroline having her finger bitten, I listened closely to the women now.

'It's the fault of people who leave their food rubbish lying around,' the first one said. 'I'm glad the council's putting up new notices, warning people about dropping litter and threatening them with fines. It's about time they clamped down on it.'

'Yes, and on the people who feed the gulls, too! Some holidaymakers think they're being kind, until they get swooped on and pecked. The gulls should be left to feed themselves with their natural food.'

'There are signs up now about that too,' said the other woman. '*Please Do Not Feed the Gulls. They are Becoming a Nuisance.* I just hope it works, otherwise Mudditon is never going to recover from this year's slump in bookings.' She paused, and I suddenly realised she was looking straight at me. I'd been so interested in what they were saying, I'd poked my head a little way out of the hiding place behind the fence where I'd been resting with the gang. 'Look at that little cat watching us,' she said, nudging her companion. 'Haven't seen him around here before.'

'No. I suppose he's one of the ferals, but he doesn't seem as nervous as most of them, does he, Jean? Hello, puss!'

I shrank back behind the fence. Big was growling at me.

'Stay out of sight, Charlie, for catnip's sake! I keep telling you – *you* might like humans, but they don't like us!'

'Sorry. I'm trying to listen to what they're saying. It's interesting. I'll tell you in a minute.'

'Well, I know some people think they're a nuisance,' the first woman went on, 'but the feral cats do have their uses.'

'Do they? I can't think what, although I do feel sorry for them.'

'Well, there was a bit in the local paper this week about how they prowl around at night, foraging for food in the streets and around the bins. They're actually keeping down the amount of food waste, Shirley. I'd sooner the wild cats ate the leftovers people throw away, than the seagulls, and hopefully in the end they'll give up, if there isn't enough food lying around for them, and they'll go back to eating their natural diet.'

'Yes, that's true, I suppose. And of course, the cats keep down the numbers of rats and mice, too. It's a shame they can't catch the odd seagull! Or at least chase them away. Then we'd really have cause to be grateful to them.'

'Yes, and perhaps the council would stop threatening to exterminate the poor things. They should realise they're actually performing a public service!'

Their conversation turned to something less interesting then, so I turned back to the other cats and related what I'd overheard.

'She actually said we perform a public service?' Black meowed in surprise.

'I thought all the humans hated us,' said Tail-less.

'Well, it seems like some of them, at least, realise that you're helping to keep the seagulls away by getting to the food waste before they do,' I said. 'Of course, if you could *catch* seagulls, or chase them off, you'd make yourselves really popular, but that's not going to happen, is it.'

There was a silence.

'You're surely not going to tell me you can catch seagulls?' I said in disbelief. 'They're huge! And scary!'

'Sadly, that's something even we wouldn't attempt,' Big said. 'But chasing them away? We haven't tried that yet. What do you think, boys? Might be a bit of fun!'

'Are you mad?' I said. 'They've got those massive great beaks. They'll turn on you and take a bite out of your faces!'

'Not if we all charge at them together,' Stinky said. 'We're quite a force, when we work as a team, Charlie.'

'I know,' I said, giving my wounded paw a little lick. 'Tell me about it. But *seagulls*? Really?'

'Worth a try, isn't it?' Black said. 'If it means the humans around here would leave us alone and stop throwing things at us.'

'Right, that's settled,' said Big. 'We'll get up a bit earlier than usual tomorrow, boys, and see what we can do. You can watch, Charlie. Don't get me wrong, I know you're a lot tougher than you look, after the way you came back for *me* the other day. But you're still injured. You might be able to help when that leg heals up, but meanwhile just watch and learn.'

Despite my constant worries about finding Caroline and my futile attempts to find the holiday cottage, I must admit I fell asleep that night feeling ever so slightly proud of myself. I was learning to scavenge. I was learning to steal fish. I was going to learn to chase seagulls. I was tough, I was brave – I was surviving. For a minute I'd almost forgotten I didn't want to become like the ferals.

Over the next couple of days, between continuing the search for my holiday home and practising chasing seagulls, our little gang was kept busy. To begin with, they only chased one solitary gull at a time, picking them when they were engrossed in feeding on something dropped on the pavement, or strutting towards humans eating on the beach. It was satisfying to see the look of alarm in their beady eyes as they took off, shouting at us crossly. Gradually they progressed to chasing off three or four at a time, and by then I was so caught up in the excitement, I couldn't resist joining in. The five of us would rush them at once, and so far we'd escaped any injuries so we were beginning to feel invincible. Inevitably, though, there came the time when, occupied with chasing off two fat gulls coming in to land on the beach, we didn't notice one of their friends running up behind us. Flapping his huge wings, he forced poor Stinky to the ground and began pecking him viciously.

'Get off me!' he screamed, trying in vain to fight back with his claws and teeth.

Within seconds the rest of us were rushing at the gull, who gave one disgusted 'Caw' and took off to follow his friends.

'Are you OK, Stinky?' I asked. I was secretly pretty pleased with myself for joining in with his rescue without a second thought for my own safety, despite my injured leg. I was becoming braver and more heroic by the day!

'Just a few scratches,' he said, getting to his paws.

But after we'd all calmed down, I noticed him wiping blood from his head and licking a sore area of his flank where the fur had been pulled out.

'I'll kill that seagull for you if he comes near us again,' I told him.

'Nice thought, Charlie, boy,' he said. 'But it'd take more than one of you.'

If nothing else, the incident had reminded us all about the wisdom of keeping very close together.

Normally we'd make ourselves scarce as soon as we'd got rid of the gulls, before any humans on the beach could pay too much attention to us, as the other boys still had an instinctive distrust of them. But on a couple of occasions, as we darted back out of sight behind a rocky outcrop where we could lie in wait, there was a burst of noise from various humans who'd been watching us.

'What's that?' Tail-less asked nervously the first time it happened.

'They're cheering,' I said. 'And clapping – banging their front paws together. They do it when they're pleased.'

'Really?' said Big. 'I thought they sounded fierce.'

'No. They're telling us we did a good job.' I looked around at the others. 'See? It's just as we hoped. The humans are on our side when it comes to chasing the seagulls away from their picnics.'

This seemed to spur my friends on. It was as if we were on a mission: every time we saw a gull anywhere near humans, or looking as if it was going to start helping itself to human food, we scared it away.

'Let's hope those pesky gulls get the message in the end,' Stinky said. 'We don't want them on our patch.'

And so it was that for the remainder of my time with the ferals, we dispersed more seagulls from the town than any cats anywhere could ever have done before. We were strong, we were powerful, we were fearless and undefeatable. Before long, we could see we were really making a difference, starting to keep the area free of scavenging seagulls and pleasing the human population, who on the whole were becoming kinder towards us.

I was particularly aware of this because of listening to the conversations of the two females called Jean and Shirley. Unknown to Big – who would definitely have tried to stop me – I'd started hanging around the café where they seemed to meet every day. They'd noticed me outside the fence again, and had called out hello to me in such friendly voices, I knew they were kind humans who wouldn't hurt me. I was desperate for some human affection, and I knew Big wouldn't understand. So I waited until he was having a nap, and went back to the café on my own. This time when Jean noticed me and said 'Here he is again! Hello, little tabby cat. You're a friendly one, aren't you?' – I scampered up to her and wound myself around her legs.

'Ah, he's really quite tame,' Shirley crooned, reaching down to stroke me. 'And he only looks young, Jean, not much more than a kitten. Perhaps he isn't a feral after all.'

'But look at the state of him. He's definitely been fighting – and his coat's in a terrible state. Poor little thing. How come you're so friendly?' Jean added, as I started to purr with the contentment of being stroked.

'Because I'm not feral! I'm a pet, and I'm lost,' I meowed, rubbing my head against her hand.

'Perhaps he's actually a lost pet,' Shirley said, as if I hadn't just been telling her that.

'I don't know,' Jean said, looking at me doubtfully. 'If he is, I reckon he's been living rough for most of his life.'

'Someone must be feeding him, then, unless he's just hunting mice and birds.'

'Or else he's living on scraps, like all the other ferals – and helping to keep those dratted gulls away,' Jean said, and then she laughed, and added, 'although I can't imagine this little chap chasing a seagull like the others have been doing, can you, Shirley?'

I felt a bit offended, then. Little did they know, I was getting as good at it as any of them! Anyway I didn't hang around for much longer – I was too worried that Big would wake up and come looking for me, and I could just imagine how he'd feel about me not only fraternising with strange humans, but letting them stroke me. But I felt a bit better for having made friends with them, and I was determined to come back again whenever I could. It was, after all, how I got information for the other boys about what humans were saying. And, eventually, it was how I came to be taken home to my family. But that's another story, and I can see there are some small kittens among you getting sleepy. So I think we should probably say goodnight for now, and I'll tell you all about it tomorrow.

CHAPTER
THIRTEEN

Morning, everyone. I hope you're all feeling bright-eyed and bushy-tailed today? No? What's up? Oh, you didn't get much sleep, Smudge? Or you, Oliver? Nancy? *None* of you could get to sleep, could you … for worrying about the end of my story, wondering how I finally got brought home again? Well, I'm sorry, I must say. Imagine how *I* felt, wondering about it myself, night after night, curled up in that nook in the brick wall with Big snoring next to me. I might have gone a little bit feral myself in some ways, but I never quite got used to not having a soft, comfy bed to sleep in. So think yourselves lucky! I shall never take my good fortune for granted again, I can assure you.

One of the things that bothered me most during those long, uncomfortable nights, when I was often sleepless with homesickness and anxiety about the future, was that my family would be getting used to living without me. Caroline might have forgotten about me. What if they gave up on me, and got themselves a new cat to replace me? If they saw me now, would they even recognise me? I had no doubt I'd changed since I'd been living rough. Quite apart from the scars I'd got from that fight, and the slight limp I still had because of my leg wound, I could feel that I was thinner. I was probably unhealthy-looking from my peculiar diet, too, although my muscles felt harder and stronger. My fur was getting matted because, although I refused to neglect my personal hygiene, and I puzzled my new friends by insisting on washing myself thoroughly after every meal, I'd been used to having my coat cared for and brushed by my humans too. I guessed I'd be taunted and teased if I mentioned any concerns about my appearance, but I hated to think that I'd probably also got fleas by now. All the boys spent so much time scratching themselves, I had to accept it was inevitable, and started to regret all the times I'd fought against Julian and Laura when they'd been administering flea treatments to the back of my neck. We really should show more appreciation of how much our humans do for us, you know, but of course, we cats prefer to think we could manage without them. I've learnt my lesson the hard way. I always thought they needed us more than we need them, but in fact – I hate to say it, and you might not believe it – but the reverse is probably true.

Another thing I missed was *playing*. It probably sounds strange, but feral cats don't play, not once they've grown out of their kittenhood, anyway. Their lives are too dangerous, too hard, and they have enough to do, trying to get food and keep safe from predators. Ah, don't cry for them, Tabitha. They don't know any different, remember. They've never had humans getting down on a nice soft carpet with them and rolling balls to them or tickling them, never had presents of toy mice filled with catnip … All right, I'm making you all upset now, I can see, so I'll move on. But, you see, *I* missed it. I missed just having the freedom to leap around in the sunshine, chasing my tail or my shadow or some fluttery butterflies. After all, I was still only half grown. Now you know what I meant at the beginning of my story when I said I'd had to grow up fast.

Walking the streets day after day with one or more of the gang, trying to find the part of town where I'd been staying with my family, I was getting more and more dispirited. I knew I needed to find the holiday cottage before they moved back to Little Broomford, otherwise how on earth would I ever find them again? But I had no idea how much time had passed, and whether in fact they might have gone back already. Even if Caroline *hadn't* forgotten about me, I hated to think of her missing me as much as I was missing her. And what if all the worries had proved true, about her being ill again? Or what if they hadn't been able to make her head better at the hospital? I meowed to myself in distress at the thought of poor Caroline lying in bed, sick or in pain, without me there to cuddle up to her. Even if my family had left Mudditon now, I couldn't give up searching for the cottage – it was my only link with them here. What else could I do?

'I'm beginning to forget what my holiday home looked like,' I admitted sadly one day to Big. 'I'm not sure I'd know it now, if I saw it.'

'Well, you know you're welcome to stay with us permanently,' he said. 'You've fitted in really well. I'd never have thought it, when we first met. You're almost one of us now.'

He was being kind, and I rubbed my face against his to show I appreciated it, but I don't think he really meant it. I was doing my best, but I'd never quite be able to embrace their lifestyle. I was too fastidious, my accent still too genteel, and I couldn't share their obsessive interest in female cats. And more to the point, however kind he was, and however much I could feel myself gradually changing, becoming more like my new friends and less like the little kitten I'd been before, staying with the feral cats permanently was obviously not what I wanted. I wanted to go home. I wanted my old life back. I just didn't know how to make it happen.

But to pay them back for their friendship, I continued to act as their Human language translator, and I was able to report to them that there was a lot more talk around the town about our campaign against the seagulls. On one occasion, when I managed to sneak back to see my two human friends outside the café again, I found the one called Shirley reading a newspaper.

'Look at this in the local paper, Jean,' she said suddenly. *'Wild cats chase seagulls off Mudditon beach. "They saved our toddler from attack" says local mum Claire, 32. "The feral cats are doing a good job. Let them stay!"'*

'You see?' said Shirley. 'I told you the cats were helpful in their way. Good for them. I'm glad people are taking notice. I never liked seeing those poor starving cats being persecuted.'

I'd been listening from behind the fence up till then, but now I decided it was time to join them again.

'Talking of poor starving cats,' said Jean when I trotted towards them, 'here's our little tabby friend again, Shirley.'

'Ah, he seems to have adopted us!' Shirley said as I rubbed against her legs, purring.

'Yes. He certainly seems too friendly to be a feral.'

'But he isn't wearing a collar, Jean.'

I was only half listening at this point, as I'd found a little bit of cake that someone had dropped under the table, and was intent on gobbling it up.

'Look at him eating those crumbs, though!' Jean said. 'He must be absolutely starving, poor thing. Is there any milk left in the jug?'

At the mention of milk, as you can imagine, I let out a huge meow and, throwing caution to the wind, jumped straight up onto Jean's lap.

'Oh!' she said, making a surprised noise that turned into a laugh. 'He must have smelt it!'

She was pouring milk from a little white jug into a saucer. I tried to get my head under her arm so that I could drink it, but she held me back, saying 'Careful, little cat! You'll spill it!' and she put the saucer down on the ground instead.

'There you go, boy,' she said, as I jumped off her lap again and began gulping up the milk furiously.

'Thank you, that was delicious,' I meowed. 'Have you got any more?'

But they both just watched me, laughing, as I washed my whiskers.

'He's so sweet,' Shirley said. 'I'm tempted to take him home with me, you know. He's just crying out for some love and care.'

I froze on the spot. They were nice humans, and I was grateful for the milk, of course, but I didn't like the sound of this. If they took me home, they might want to keep me. And then what? I'd *never* get back to Little Broomford or see Caroline again.

'Goodbye,' I said. 'Thanks again.' Well, I didn't want to appear ungrateful. But I ran back to the yard where my friends were dozing in the sunshine, and lay down next to Big, feeling slightly ashamed now of my secret visits. It wasn't fair that I'd had a lovely dish of milk and hadn't been able to share it with them, but I knew they'd have been too afraid to trust Jean and Shirley.

I tried to make up for it by telling them later that I'd overheard some humans talking about the report in the newspaper while they were asleep. I emphasised the part about people calling for feral cats to be allowed to stay. This was all good news to my friends, of course. Not that they ever lost their distrust of humans in general, but they began to understand that not all of them were intent on hurting them or getting rid of them.

Everything started to change a couple of days later, because of a woman with a chocolate ice cream.

She was quite an elderly human, one of those whose fur have gone white and hobble along holding a stick in one paw. Why they don't just give up and walk on four paws when they get too old to balance on two, I'll never understand, but there it is. The boys and I were patrolling the seafront on the other side of the harbour this particular day. We'd already seen off a few seagulls, and had attracted the attention of a group of holiday humans who stood watching us, exclaiming and cheering us on. This old woman came tottering along with her stick, and in the other paw she had a chocolate ice cream, the type they eat out of a pointy biscuity thing, with a stick of chocolate poking out of it. My mouth watered as I watched her licking it, remembering how much Caroline loved those, and how she sometimes gave me the last bit to finish off. I wondered if I'd ever get to enjoy that kind of treat again.

Suddenly there was a shout from the crowd: 'Watch out, love!'

A huge seagull had swooped down from a lamppost and was aiming straight for the woman, trying to grab her ice cream. Suddenly I had a flashback to the day I'd watched Caroline being attacked on the beach for her sandwiches. I pictured Caroline's poor bleeding finger again, remembered how she'd fallen, and the noise she'd made when her head hit the rock. How she lay there, lifeless, for a minute, before opening her eyes and looking so ill. I let out a little mew of anguish. Where was my poor Caroline now? Perhaps she was still at the hospital – I had no idea what they did at these places, except what Oliver had told me about Caroline being in one when she was very ill before, and that they'd kept her there a long time, trying to make her better. Perhaps this time they hadn't even been able to make her better – it was bad enough her seeming to be ill again, without having got so badly hurt that day on the beach. And it was all the fault of a nasty, spiteful seagull – just like this one who was going for the poor old female's ice cream! Overcome with fury at seagulls in general, I didn't even stop to consider whether the rest of the gang was behind me, or whether in fact they'd even noticed the poor old human's desperate situation at all. I just charged forward, hissing and spitting for all I was worth.

Of course, the other boys quickly came after me, Big shouting at me for not staying with them. I like to think I got the gull pretty flustered on my own, jumping up at him and yowling my head off, but once I had the gang's support he didn't need telling anymore. He flapped away crossly without having nabbed the chocolate ice cream. The poor human had dropped it on the ground, though, as she stumbled, letting go of her stick, and she was only saved from falling over by a couple of young male humans who rushed to help her.

'Well done, Charlie,' Big said gruffly, as between us all we quickly licked up as much of the ice cream off the pavement as we could. No point in it going to waste and, as you know, humans are far too pernickety to eat off the ground. 'But it was a bit daft, wasn't it, not waiting for us? For the love of catnip, don't you realise that gull could have had your eye out?'

I flinched. One eye was already still quite sore and swollen. The thought of the other one being pecked out by a seagull was enough to make me realise how lucky I'd been, and how foolhardy. I'd landed badly on my wounded leg too, with all that jumping up at the gull.

'Sorry,' I said. 'I just felt so cross, I got carried away.'

'It was bloody brave of you, young Charlie,' said Black, coming to rub his face against mine. 'I don't think I'd have dared go for that gull on my own. Good for you.'

This was praise indeed, coming from Black. He was the most aggressive of the boys and I hadn't forgotten that he'd been the first one to attack me, that day when I'd been alone and defenceless. Up till now I'd always believed he still looked down on me somewhat as a naive, posh little house kitten.

'Thank you,' I purred. 'Thank you all,' I added as the other boys joined in with the congratulations. I looked around at them all. My new friends. I finally felt completely accepted by them now. I should be able to confide in them, shouldn't I – explain why I'd suddenly been able to behave so bravely. 'It was because of Caroline, you see – my human kitten,' I said. 'I told you she got attacked by a seagull, didn't I?'

'So what?' Stinky said.

'Well, she hurt herself – badly. Her poor head was broken, and bleeding, and she might still be in hospital, and she might be very ill, everyone's worried about her, and … and I miss her so much, she's my favourite human in the whole world, and I just want to go home to her again and find out if she's all right, and…'

I stopped. All the boys were staring at me. I realised I'd been making a terrible mewing noise at the back of my throat all through this long meow – that in fact I was probably sounding more like a pathetic baby kitten than a brave seagull-chaser.

'Sorry,' I said. 'But that was what made me so cross with that seagull.'

'Well, at least something good came of it, then!' Black said cheerfully.

They all turned away, and I tried to calm myself down again. It had been pointless, after all, trying to explain to them how I felt about Caroline. They'd never understand.

But just then, Big turned back again, breaking away from the others, and he came over to me and rubbed his face against mine. He didn't say anything. He probably didn't have a clue what to say, probably hadn't even followed a single word of my meow. But he was showing he cared – and that, for now, was something. For now, it had to be enough. But after that day, I was even more determined I'd somehow find Caroline again, even if it took me the rest of my nine lives.

CHAPTER
FOURTEEN

There was one thing about the Chocolate Ice Cream Incident that I didn't tell the others. Never having lived with humans, the feral boys had no understanding about the kind of toys they played with. So it would have been hard to explain to them that I knew people in the crowd watching us that day, and probably other days too, had been taking photos of us. I'd glimpsed them holding their phones and cameras up in the air and aiming them at us as we stalked the gulls before a chase, so it wasn't too much of a surprise to me to find out eventually that someone had captured a picture of me going to the rescue of the Ice Cream woman. This is how I found out.

Once again it was because of my new human friends Jean and Shirley. When I made my secret visits to them at the café, I often heard them talking about whatever had been written in their newspaper. On this particular occasion, a day or two after the Battle for the Chocolate Ice Cream, they were sitting with their heads close together, laughing, apparently, at a picture in it.

'That's so funny, Jean!' the one called Shirley was saying. 'Just look at that seagull, terrified of one little cat!'

'Well, you're right about one thing, Shirl, I'll give you that – the wild cats have certainly started being a deterrent around here. I hope that poor old dear wasn't badly hurt.'

'No. My niece Holly was down on the seafront that day, as it happens, and saw the whole thing. She said the cat scared the seagull right off, and although the poor woman got a nasty shock and did drop her ice cream when she stumbled, she wasn't hurt. Someone caught her and stopped her from falling over. Apparently a lot of other cats joined in afterwards but this little one had already saved the day.' Then she picked the paper up again and held it closer to her face. 'Hang on a minute!' she said, sounding excited. 'Who does this look like to you?'

They both stared at the paper again, then at me – I was sitting by Jean's feet, where I'd been washing my whiskers after their usual treat of a saucer of milk.

'Are you saying you think it's him – our little friend here?' Jean looked back at the paper again. 'Well, you could be right, although to be fair there are probably lots of little feral tabbies like this around.'

'Well, the person who sent this picture into the paper wasn't the only one to have his camera out,' said Shirley. 'My niece told me she'd filmed the whole thing on her phone. She's going to show me when she comes round tonight. She's put it on Facebook, and YouTube apparently. She says it might go viral, whatever that means. She seems to think it'll make her famous. Kids, eh? The ideas they get into their heads!'

'It's more likely to make the little cat famous!' her friend remarked, and they both laughed.

Well, by now, as you can imagine, I was meowing my head off at them.

'It *was* me who chased the seagull away from that old lady!' I said. 'I *am* that cat!'

But Jean had folded up the paper now and they were talking about something else. And even though I jumped up on Shirley's lap and nudged her hands and arms with my head until she almost spilt her tea over me, they just gave me a little stroke and laughed at me, and nothing more was said about the picture.

When I rejoined Big and the others back at the yard, I was still so worked up about the whole thing, I couldn't resist telling him what I'd overheard.

'You mean to tell me you've been hanging around outside that café on your own while we were asleep?' he meowed at me. 'Have you suddenly got a death wish, these last few days?'

'I couldn't sleep,' I said. 'I was just listening.' I wondered if he could smell humans on me. What would he say if he knew I'd actually been cuddling up with them?

'Charlie,' he said in a stern meow, 'I keep telling you not to take risks around humans. Even if some of them might not mind us so much now, you don't know which ones might still be dangerous.'

'They were talking about *me*, though! They had a picture of me in their newspaper.'

He gave me a pitying look. 'Charlie, do us all a favour, right? Don't let all the fuss about your bravery the other day go to your head. You're a good little cat, at the end of the day, but nobody likes a show off.'

'I'm not showing off!' I protested. 'I could hear what they were saying.'

'Yes, I know you can understand Human. But please, don't start telling me they've got pictures of you. That's just too far-fetched for common sense.'

I knew I'd never convince him otherwise. For a start, he didn't know about cameras and phones making pictures. Even I didn't understand how it worked, how a picture of me had got from someone's phone into the newspaper, but I did at least believe it was possible – I knew how clever humans could be with things like that. I didn't like Big thinking I was just a show off, so I just dropped the subject. But Jean's and Shirley's words lingered in my head, and in my dreams, giving me a funny, fluttery, hopeful feeling that wouldn't quite go away. Could it be true? Could the pictures from the humans' cameras really make me famous? And if they did, would it actually be such a bad thing, after all – especially if I got famous enough to be sent back home to my family?

What happened next, though, was so surprising, I still have trouble understanding it myself, even though I've learnt more about it since. There are lots of things in the human world, of course, that I still don't understand. So if any of the older cats among you can enlighten me, I'm always willing to be educated, even now I'm not a little kitten anymore.

A few days after I heard about my picture being in the newspaper, Big and I were walking along the street where all the shops were. We were once again heading to a different part of town to see if I recognised anywhere that could have been my holiday home. I remember I was feeling particularly sad, as we trotted along together, because Big had just asked me whether I should be thinking about giving up now. I'd already suspected that a couple of the boys were getting tired of helping me with the search, but Big was very loyal to me, and had said he'd keep on coming out with me for as long as I wanted to. I guessed he just thought that by giving up I could spare myself more disappointment. But how could I ever give up looking for Caroline and the rest of my family? It would feel like I'd forgotten them and stopped caring about them, and that was never going to happen.

I was getting to know the shops. There were the ones selling food, of course, where the windows were full of bread and cakes, or those boring things humans eat that grow on trees or bushes, and of course there was our favourite, the shop that displayed delicious looking body parts of dead prey, and whole chickens hanging up on hooks. Other shops were less interesting. They had humans' clothes in the windows, or shoes, or books, or toys for human kittens. Then right at the end of the row of shops was one with lots of televisions in the window. If there weren't any humans hanging around outside, we sometimes loitered here for a few minutes because the televisions were usually turned on, showing various different pictures, and Big and the other cats found them fascinating. They had no idea what televisions were, of course, never having been inside a human house. I'd tried to explain, but of course like all of us I've never really understood the need for them myself.

'You mean they just sit there and watch these things all the time?' Stinky had retorted when I first told him my family had two of them in our proper home at Little Broomford.

'Well, mostly in the evenings, but yes, they can watch them whenever they want to. Sometimes there are special pictures for human kittens to watch. And sometimes there are pictures of lots of male humans chasing each other and kicking a ball. I've noticed that if I walk in front of the television waving my tail, they sometimes tell me off. But if the picture is of something like birds or fish, and I sit on the shelf on top of it and dangle a paw over it, they find it quite funny.'

'Suffering catnip!' Black had said. 'Humans are the weirdest creatures in the world.'

'And the pictures keep moving!' Big had said.

'Yes. I suppose it gives them some sort of a thrill, like us watching a bird hopping, or a mouse creeping along.'

'But at least we eventually pounce on the prey and eat it,' one of the boys had said, and I'd had to agree, the whole thing about watching television really did seem like a pointless exercise to us.

This particular day, it was raining, with a stiff breeze blowing up the shopping street from the sea, and most of the humans must have stayed inside their houses, so Big and I spent a while staring at the moving pictures in the shop window. One of the television screens was showing pictures of almost naked humans swimming in a big bath of water. When the first one reached the edge of the bath, he threw both his front paws into the air and the humans who were watching stood up and clapped their paws together. Very strange. On another screen, there were pictures of pairs of humans holding on to each other and swaying together in very strange, unnatural looking positions. The females were wearing fancy flamboyant dresses so I could only surmise that the smartly dressed males were trying to stop them from tripping over.

'It's true,' I commented to Big now. 'The longer I'm away from my humans, the more I agree that they're all a bit odd.'

And then I looked at the next television screen. And I nearly jumped with all four paws off the ground.

'Oh my claws and whiskers!' I meowed. I was beginning to pick up some of the boys' vernacular. 'It's me! Big, look, it's *me* on there, for the love of catnip!'

'It can't be!' Big was staring at the same screen now. 'It must be some other tabby with the same eyes...' He glanced at my still slightly swollen right eye. 'And the same scars on his head ... and ... oh. The same limp when he runs. That's a coincidence. And...' He broke off. 'Bloody catnip, Charlie! It's *you*!'

We both stared at the picture on the screen as it continued to show me running forwards across the pavement and then leaping into the air, and then the seagull flying off with an angry squawk and the old lady stumbling, dropping her chocolate ice cream, and being helped by the two young humans.

'It's me,' I repeated.

'It is,' he agreed, turning to stare at me now. 'How in the name of all the dogs and foxes did you do that?'

'I didn't do anything! It's ... I don't know! Somehow my life has got repeated in pictures on that television.'

'That's impossible! You haven't been inside that shop, have you?'

'No, of course I haven't. I don't understand it any more than you do. I told you I think someone has put a picture of me in a newspaper, but...'

'Yes, and that was unbelievable enough – I thought you were making it up. But *this*...' He stared back at the shop window again, where the television screen was now just showing a male human with his mouth opening and closing as if he was talking to us, with a lot of Human writing running along the bottom of the screen. 'This is just *impossible*. It defies all common sense.'

'I know. But it was definitely me, wasn't it. It was me jumping up at that seagull.'

'Yes, it was, although if I hadn't seen it with my own eyes I'd say you'd finally taken leave of your senses.'

We stayed there in the rain, with the wind whistling around our whiskers, for quite a long time after that, in case we saw the pictures of me again, but it didn't happen. In the end we waited so long, we got drenching wet and cold, and didn't bother with searching for my holiday home that day after all.

'Let's not tell the other boys what we saw in that shop,' Big said quietly as we headed back to the yard. 'They'll think we've both been at the catnip.'

'OK,' I agreed. I was beginning to wonder if I'd dreamt it, anyway. It all seemed so unreal and unlikely. 'But we *did* see it, though, didn't we?'

'Yes.' He turned to stare at me again. 'And I'm still trying to make sense of it. The only thing I can think of is that you've got some kind of magic power – what with this, and understanding Human, and the way you were brave enough to come back and attack me, all on your own, that first day we met. It never did seem quite natural. Are you sure you're really a normal cat?'

'Yes, I am!' I meowed, feeling a bit scared now.

I had no idea what had happened there. But if I'd really had magic powers, there was one thing I was sure of: I'd have magicked myself back to my human family by now and would be sitting on Caroline's lap, purring into her ear, and not caring if she spent all day every day looking at strange moving pictures on the television, just as long as I never lost her again.

The following day, we were walking past the pub at the harbour when we saw another strange thing. Inside the pub window was a big piece of paper with a picture of a cat on it and some large Human writing underneath. This time it was Tail-less who noticed.

'Blinking codfish, Charlie!' he meowed. 'That cat in the picture looks just like you!'

Big, still feeling spooked by what we'd seen on the television screen, immediately crept up for a closer look.

'It *does* look like you,' he told me, almost accusingly, when he came back, 'but I don't think it is. That cat looks fatter, and more groomed, and it hasn't got scars on its head or a nasty eye, like you.'

'Right,' I said. Even from a little distance, I could see it was true that the cat in the picture didn't have my wounds.

Of course, I wasn't sure exactly what I looked like, apart from what my humans, and other cats, had told me. Caroline had sometimes picked me up and held me in front of that shiny thing they call a mirror, and said things like 'Ah, Charlie, look at you!' – but all I could see was the little tabby kitten who always seemed to appear in the mirrors around the house, copying whatever I was doing. When I was very young, I thought he was another kitten who lived in the house, but Ollie soon put me right on that, explaining that he wasn't real – he had no scent and if I tried to rub faces with him, all I'd get was the hard shiny surface of the mirror. I presume you all think the same as Ollie and I do – that the mirror cats are something like the pictures on television.

So the mirror cat in our house may, perhaps, have been a picture of me. If it was, then I had a good idea what I used to look like before I got lost and started living rough. Before I got badly beaten up by a gang of alley cats, almost lost the sight in one eye and apparently gained some scars that I supposed would last my whole nine lives. But I didn't want to freak Big out any more than I'd done already.

'OK. Obviously not me, then,' I said.

We saw another picture, exactly the same, in the café window. Another one in the window of the fish and chip shop when we went scavenging that evening. Next day, there was one in the bookshop, one in the bread shop, and one in the window of the Chinese takeaway shop. When we walked back past the café, Shirley and Jean were sitting in their usual spot outside. I lingered behind the fence for a while to listen to their conversation, and Big waited for me. He didn't mind me using my two friends as sources of inside information, as long as he was there to keep an eye on me and I didn't venture too close.

'It's such a shame, isn't it,' Shirley was saying. 'They must be so desperate to get him back. The pictures are going up everywhere.'

'Yes. Well, of course, since it was on the News, everyone knows about that cat who chased the seagull away from the old lady. The family who put up the notices seem to be convinced it's their cat, don't they? They were staying here all through August, I heard – down at the Oversands end of the bay, in one of those rental cottages, apparently. The little girl's inconsolable. There's some story about her being very ill, and she seems to think it's her fault the cat went missing.'

'Ah, bless her, poor little love. And that's her little cat in the picture, is it, Jean?'

'Yes. Look, have you read it? *LOST: CHARLIE. Young neutered male tabby. Last seen on 28 August in the Oversands area of Mudditon-on-Sea. Believed to be still in Mudditon. Microchipped. Reward for safe return.* And it's got a mobile number and email address. Apparently the girl's father has been staying in Mudditon again since they saw the cat on the News – walking the streets, calling out for Charlie.'

'Well, I do hope he finds him, for that little girl's sake. If it is that same cat, of course. Tabby cats are two a penny, though, aren't they? For a start, there's our little friend who visits us here. He's a tabby, and he looks about the right age, doesn't he. And we did think he looked like the cat who was in the paper.'

'Yes, but come on, Shirl – he's much skinnier than this one in the poster, and so scruffy looking, poor little thing. He really doesn't look like this cute kitten in the pictures, at all. To be honest, I wonder if the family are just clutching at straws. I'd be very surprised if the cat in these posters is the same one who chased the seagull.'

'But then again, we've both been saying our little one doesn't really behave like a feral, haven't we. He seems too trusting.'

I'm sure you can imagine how I felt as I listened to all this! I was mewing to myself like crazy and twitching all over with distress.

'What the dog's bum is up with you?' Big kept asking me, but I was too intent on listening, to reply. Julian was looking for me! It seemed that so much time had passed, my family must have actually gone home to Little Broomford, but they hadn't forgotten me. Caroline was pining for me! Julian had come back specially to put up pictures of me, he was walking the streets calling me! If only he would walk past here right now, I'd run to him, and I'd be rescued. I'd be taken home, I'd see Caroline, I'd be back to my old life, to you, Oliver, and you, all my other old friends in Little Broomford.

But then I mewed again with a new bout of anguish. What if he never happened to walk along the same street or path or alleyway at the same time as me? What if he gave up, like Big had suggested I ought to give up looking for the holiday cottage? Then he'd go back home without me, telling Caroline I was nowhere to be found. The pictures would be taken down again, and all the humans around here would stop talking about me the way Jean and Shirley were doing now, and nobody would look for me, and I'd have lost my only opportunity of going back to my real life. How could I afford to take that chance?

I glanced at Big. He was looking at me with such concern, meowing quietly to me about calming down and not getting myself upset, and why didn't I tell him what the humans were saying? And I felt yet another wave of distress as I realised how fond I'd become of him and the other boys, how they'd taken me into their gang and looked after me, despite the fact that I was so different from them, and despite them thinking I was weird and posh and possibly magic on top of everything else. They'd be upset with me for leaving them now. Or perhaps they wouldn't – perhaps they'd just think that was part of my weirdness, and forget about me as quickly as they'd accepted me.

'Well,' Jean was saying, 'even if it really is our little cat, Shirl, there's not a lot we can do until we see him again – then we could have another good look at him. Now, shall we get the bill? I need to get back and start a bit of housework.'

So this was it. I had to trust those two females; trust them, and trust my own grasp of Human language, or my chance was gone. I poised myself, preparing to make a dash for it.

'Where are you going, Charlie?' Big said, but there was something in his voice that made me think he'd guessed this was goodbye.

'I'm sorry, Big,' I meowed. 'Thanks for everything. Say goodbye to the boys for me. I'll miss you all.'

'Charlie!' he yowled as I ran straight round the end of the fence and threw myself at the legs of the nearest of the two females. 'For the love of bloody rats' intestines, don't do it! They'll skin you alive! They'll roast you and eat you with their stinky red ketchup!'

'Goodbye, Big,' I mewed back to him loudly, as Shirley, gasping with surprise and squawking to Jean about what a coincidence it was that I'd turned up at that very moment, bent down to pick me up. 'I'm really sorry,' I called back as he continued to yowl after me 'But I'm going home.'

CHAPTER
FIFTEEN

It wasn't until I was being held tightly in the arms of this human female I'd adopted as my friend, that I realised just how much I'd changed since I'd been living rough with the feral cats. She was squashing me against her enormous chest with her big plump arms, she was so determined not to let me go, and I was having to clench my teeth, shut my eyes tight and force myself to lie still, so strong was my instinct to nip her sharply on her wrist, jump down and run away. But even while I was struggling with myself I was wondering how it was that I seemed to have lost my trust in humans. I'd never been frightened of them in the old days. Oliver had taught me that although there were definitely some bad ones in the world, most of them were kind to us cats and wanted to be our friends. Yes, I've always remembered that, Ollie, because I was impressed that you'd learned to trust humans again despite having had a horrible experience with a very cruel human when you were a tiny kitten.

I was thinking about this now, telling myself to remember Oliver's wise words, as Shirley was holding me in her tight grip.

'Isn't this incredible, Jean?' she was saying. 'Just as we were talking about him, he turned up!'

'Yes, it's amazing,' agreed Jean, 'it's almost as if he was sat behind the fence listening to our whole conversation.'

'I wonder if he *is* the missing Charlie. You're right, though, he's not like the picture in the poster. His coat is in a terrible state, and he's got a few battle scars. And I don't like the look of that poor eye.'

'Well, the poster says he's microchipped, so there's only one way to find out whether it's him,' said Jean.

'Yes!' I meowed urgently. 'The only way is to take me to Julian! He'll recognise me straight away! Call his number! You said it was on that notice!'

But instead, they were fussing around, paying for their tea, getting their handbags and suddenly I was being carried off, out of the café and along the road.

'Where are we going?' I squealed, struggling furiously, as they carried me further and further away from the yard and my new friends. Even now, they'd probably be talking about me, wondering together at my stupidity in running off with humans. Would they miss me? Or would they just be glad to be rid of a nuisance and a liability?

'Calm down, little cat,' Shirley soothed me. 'We're not going to hurt you.'

'Here we are,' Jean said suddenly, stopping outside a house. There was a little car parked in front of it and she unlocked its doors. 'You sit in the back with him, Shirley. He really ought to be in a basket of some sort, but it's only a short drive. Look, I've got a little blanket there on the back seat that I use for my grandson. Let's wrap him up in that so he can't try to escape if he panics.'

'No!' I meowed, starting to wriggle frantically now as Shirley climbed awkwardly into the back of the car with me and proceeded, with Jean's help, to wrap me up so that all my paws were completely immobilised. 'Let me go!'

'There,' Jean panted. 'Now just hold his head down so he can't bite you. He's getting upset, poor little thing.'

'Of course I'm upset! You've taken me prisoner! I don't want to go in the car with you! Where are you taking me?'

All my resolve to trust Jean and Shirley and to remember Oliver's words of wisdom had flown out of the window. And as the doors were slammed shut, and Jean started the car running along, I'm ashamed to say I cowered on Shirley's lap, growling quietly and letting out the occasional little mew of fear as if I was the kind of cat who'd never been used to humans at all.

'It's all right, little kitty,' Shirley kept saying. 'It's all right.'

But it wasn't. It was all wrong. I shouldn't have trusted these humans. Why had they tied me up? What were they going to do to me? I should have listened to Big, after all, and stayed with him and the boys, where I was safe and being looked after. At the thought of Big, I mewed even more loudly. He'd been such a good friend! I'd remember him for my whole nine lives! I'd forget all about going back to Little Broomford, if only I could magic myself back with him and the boys right this minute!

Oh yes, you might very well look shocked, my friends. I can hardly believe it myself now. How appalling, how shameful that I was thinking like this, forgetting already where my real loyalties lay, forgetting how much I'd yearned for a chance to be back with my human family, to be cuddled by Caroline again and fed lovely cat food by Laura.

But this is what fear does to you. It turns you from a sensible, reasonable cat – from a hero cat, in fact, one who has survived extreme danger, who has risked lives and limbs to try to protect his vulnerable and much-loved human kitten – into a snivelling wretch of a scaredy-cat.

I admit it, I was behaving like a scaredy-cat and I'm ashamed now to think about it. After everything I'd been through, you see, it seemed like just as happiness and reunion with my humans had been within my sight, I'd ended up making the wrong choice, a fatal mistake. And now I was so frightened and alone, I felt like giving up. I just lay there and cried. I cried for Big and the other boys. I cried for Julian and Laura and Caroline and even baby Jessica. I cried for *you*, Oliver, and *you*, my sisters and friends back in Little Broomford. But mostly, I cried for myself.

Thank goodness, though, it wasn't very long before the car stopped again.

'Here we are,' Shirley said, still clutching me in my tightly wrapped bundle as Jean helped her out of the car. 'Now, don't start panicking, little kitty. Mr Caswell is a very kind man.'

Mr Caswell? Who the fox's backside was Mr Caswell? I couldn't imagine how he could be anyone kind. If these human catnappers had been genuinely on my side, they'd have been taking me straight to Julian! Anyone else could only be plotting to do me harm. Surely it couldn't be true what Big had been screaming to me? Were they going to roast me and eat me with ketchup? Oh my ears and whiskers!

I wriggled and wriggled, yowling and spitting at Shirley as she carried me up some steps into a building that smelt … it smelt like … what *was* that smell? What was the memory it was bringing back to me? It was making me shudder, would have made my fur stand on end and my muscles quiver, if only there was room for that to happen inside my tight bundle. We went through a door into an empty room with a bare floor and some hard empty chairs around the walls. The smell in here was almost overpowering. And just then, another door opened and out came a dog – fortunately, attached to a human by one of those long straps they need to keep them under control – and immediately, it all came flooding back to me. I knew where we were! For catnip's sake, they'd brought me to a vet!

Can you imagine how much I was wriggling and hissing and spitting now? Shirley almost dropped me twice, and Jean had to help her to hang onto me.

'Let me go,' I growled. And to the dog, who was sniffing around their feet, trying to jump at their legs to get a closer look at me, I shouted: 'Bugger off, you big stupid snarling piece of rat's poo, you!'

I know, I know, my language was pretty awful. It was the influence of the feral boys, you see, together with the terror of my situation. I couldn't help it. But I don't speak like that anymore, now I'm back in civilisation, obviously, so please don't let the little kittens here copy me.

'Down, boy!' the dog's human was trying to persuade him. 'You're frightening the poor cat. Sorry, ladies,' he said to my captors. 'That's a feisty little feline you've got there!'

'Oh, he's not ours,' Jean said. 'We think he's a feral, although we did wonder if he might be a stray – the one who's been advertised in all the shops and cafés. We're hoping the vet can scan him, even if just to rule it out.'

'No!' I shrieked, trying to get my teeth into Shirley's wrist. 'I know what vets do – I'm not stupid! He'll stick a needle in me! It'll put me to sleep! I'll never wake up!'

And just at that moment, the other door opened again and out came a tall male human in a white coat.

'Hello,' he said to the females. 'Have you got an appointment?'

'No,' Jean said, still trying to help Shirley to hang onto me. She could hardly make herself heard above my yowling. 'Sorry, Mr Caswell, it's kind of an emergency.'

'Has he been hurt or something?' said the male, peering down at me. I spat in his face.

'No, we've found him,' Shirley said. 'Well, he actually found us! We did wonder whether he might be the missing cat that's in all the posters around town. I hope so, anyway, now we've gone to all this trouble,' she added with a little laugh. 'Although he's been so feisty on the way here, I'm beginning to think he is a feral after all.'

'Oh yes, I've got one of those posters up myself,' the vet said, still staring at me. 'His owner, a Mr Smythe, came in to tell me about him. The cat was on the BBC News, apparently – chased a seagull, or something?'

'That's right. Do you think it's him, Mr Caswell?' Jean asked.

'I doubt it, to be honest. As you say, this cat seems half wild. Let's have a look at him, anyway, shall we? Bring him through. I'll get Ginny to help me hold him still. We're going to need our gloves on, I think!'

And so, as the human with the dog went out, calling, 'Good luck. I hope it is the missing cat,' I was carried through to the next room. In here, the smell reminded me so strongly of my previous experiences with vets that I nearly fainted. I was unwrapped onto one of those slippery, shiny tables, where I was forcibly held down by Mr Caswell on one side, and a young female in a white coat on the other. I'd stopped yowling now. I was so sick with fear, I'd kind of retreated inside myself and just lay panting, waiting for the end of my lives.

'He's certainly quite a young cat,' the vet said, having prised open my mouth and looked at my teeth. 'A neutered male, probably only about a year old. Very malnourished.' He was poking me around the ribs. 'Covered in fleas. Coat dull and matted. One back leg injured – he seems to have had a bite down to the bone that hasn't healed properly and it's left him with an abscess.' I flinched as he touched my sore leg. 'Sorry, boy. Scabs on his head, one ear bitten, and a very badly infected right eye. Lucky not to have lost his sight. Been in a few fights, by the look of him. Well, ladies, I'd be surprised if this is our missing Charlie. I'd say he's more likely to be a long-term stray who's turned feral. But I'll certainly scan him for you to make sure. If it's not him, we'll keep him here, treat his wounds, de-flea him and get him nursed back to health, and send him to Cats' Protection. Hopefully someone will adopt him.'

I wasn't listening anymore. His Human words were all running into each other, making no sense to me. I'd switched off. I was waiting for that needle, and just hoping the end would be quick.

'Pass me the scanner,' he said to the nurse, and the next thing I knew, something cold was being run over the back of my neck. *Here comes the needle*, I thought. *Oh well, this is it. Goodbye, cruel world. Goodbye, Caroline. Goodbye, Laura, Julian* ... but before I'd even finished my litany of farewells, the vet was speaking again. I tried to concentrate this time, to tune in and hear what he was saying. It might be the last thing I ever heard, after all.

'Would you ladies mind holding him on this side, while I check the computer?'

Jean and Shirley grabbed hold of me together. There was silence, apart from some tapping noises as Mr Caswell did something on his computer. And then:

'Well I never! That *is* a surprise. You're quite right, ladies. Well done – you have found our missing hero!'

Hero? Was he talking about me? Was he not going to kill me, then? I tried to lift my head to look at him. He was smiling.

'Poor Charlie, eh! He must have really been through it these past few weeks to end up in this condition. Well, it's good news. I'm going to give Mr Smythe a call right now. I think he's still staying in one of the hotels down at the seafront. He told me he's taken a week off work and was going to search the town day and night until he found this little chap. His daughter is inconsolable, apparently, breaking her heart over him.'

'Oh, I'm so pleased we found him!' Jean said, clapping her paws together.

'Me too.' Shirley looked like she was about to start mewing.

'You're in line for a hefty reward,' the vet said to the two females as he picked up his phone, but they were both shaking their heads.

'Oh, we don't want any money, do we, Shirl?' Jean exclaimed. 'We just want Charlie taken back where he belongs.'

'That's right,' Shirley agreed, as the vet started talking on his phone. 'That poor little girl will be so happy!'

Poor little girl? Were they talking about Caroline? I tried to sit up, but they were still holding me firmly. Were they saying I *wasn't* going to be killed? No injection? No roasting and eating with ketchup? Could it really be true?

'Am I going home?' I meowed loudly. 'Are you not going to hurt me?'

They all laughed. 'It's as if he knows he's going to be all right now,' said Jean. 'Look, he's completely settled down. I think he trusts us now.'

'I've spoken to Mr Smythe,' the vet said. 'He's on his way.' Mr Caswell came over to the table and started tickling me under the chin. 'Yes, you're a nice boy really, aren't you, Charlie?' he said very gently. 'Not a wild cat at all, just a poor little tabby who got lost.'

To my surprise, I found myself purring. I'd misjudged him. He liked me! And the two females weren't catnappers after all – they were my rescuers! I rubbed my head against their hands and purred at them too, and they all laughed again, sounding as happy as I was, now beginning to feel myself.

The young nurse lifted me down to the floor and put a bowl of lovely milk in front of me. I fell on it and lapped it all up.

'That's it, Charlie, now let's get you some food too,' she said, sounding like she was almost mewing too. 'You've had a rotten time, by the look of you, and you must be starving. But it's all over now. Your master's coming to get you. You're going home, Charlie. You're going home to your little girl!'

CHAPTER
SIXTEEN

I was asleep in a kind of cage thing in a back room of the vet's when I heard Julian's voice. I wasn't very happy about being put in the cage, just when I'd made up my mind to trust Mr Caswell and Ginny the nurse, and thought they liked me. But I'd been well fed, and after all the trauma I'd been through, I was exhausted, so I gave in, let them shut the cage door and settled down on the mat inside the cage. I was just in the middle of a very satisfying dream where I was playing with a fat frog at the edge of the big pond at home, when I heard Julian calling me.

'OK,' I meowed in my dream, 'I'll just make this frog jump one more time, then I'll come in . . .', and then I woke up with a start, looked around me, and remembered where I was. Julian was smiling at me through the door of the cage.

I jumped up, purring at the top of my lungs. I'd never been so happy to see anyone! I put my front paws up to the cage door, trying to get out, trying to lick him through the bars, meowing and purring for all I was worth.

'Hello, boy. What a welcome!' Julian said. His voice sounded wobbly.

Ginny reached around him to unlock the cage and he took hold of me, hugging me close.

'Look at the state of you,' he murmured. 'You poor little fellow.'

'Mr Caswell says he must have been living rough, and he's definitely got into a fight or two,' Ginny said. 'He was half wild with fear when the two ladies brought him in.'

'Where are they?' Julian looked around him as he carried me through to the vet's room. 'I wanted to thank them. I offered a reward.'

'They said they wouldn't accept anything,' Mr Caswell said, turning round from wiping down the table. 'They were just thrilled to bits to have found Charlie and that he would be going home safely.'

'But I *must* thank them, at least! And if they won't accept the reward, I'll send the money to a cat charity.'

'Well, I'm sure Jean and Shirley would really appreciate that. They're both cat lovers.'

'Oh, you know them? They live locally?'

'Yes. They both have pets registered here, and bring them in for their regular check-ups and so on.'

'Would you be able to give me their phone numbers, then, or is that against your data protection?'

Mr Caswell was smiling. 'It's fine, Mr Smythe. They actually asked me to give you their contact details. They asked if you'd be kind enough to update them on Charlie's recovery.'

'Of course I will,' Julian said, taking a piece of paper from the vet and putting it in his wallet. 'Now, what do I owe you?'

'Nothing *yet*, because I haven't actually started Charlie on any treatment. I was waiting to consult you about it. I'm sure you're keen to take him straight home, but he's going to need that abscess on his leg lanced as soon as possible. I could do it right now, but he'll need to wear an Elizabethan collar afterwards to stop him licking and chewing at the wound.'

'One of those big protective collars? Animals hate wearing them, don't they?'

'At first, yes, until they get used to them. But as you've got such a long journey it might not be a good idea to upset him any further today. What I'd suggest is, I'll give Charlie a quick shot of intravenous antibiotic now, and after you get him home, see your own vet about getting the abscess treated. I'll give you some antibiotic and anti-inflammatory drops for that poor eye, too. And he also needs a flea treatment. Would you like me to do that now?'

And so I was put back on the shiny table and subjected to a needle after all, as well as a dose of flea stuff on the back of my neck. Then I had something dripped into my sore eye, which made me shake my head and twitch my ears madly. But this time I wasn't screaming or quaking with fear, because my own human was holding me, whispering words of comfort in my ear and stroking me all the while it was happening.

'He's going to need some feeding up, poor little chap,' Mr Caswell commented, feeling my ribs again. 'And his coat's going to need some attention.'

'We'll see to that ourselves,' Julian said firmly.

'Yes, I think that's best. With a bit of grooming he'll be back to his old self, and it'll help him settle back at home and bond with the family again. Although,' he added, watching as I climbed up Julian's chest and tried to bury myself inside his shirt, 'from what I can see, I suspect that's not going to be a problem.'

Julian laughed, but Mr Caswell lowered his voice and added, 'Just a word of warning. Keep a close eye on him. There's just a chance he might have picked up something more serious, if he was involved in any fights with feral cats. They can carry disease in their saliva, which can be transferred in a bite. I'm sure your own vet will advise you. He might want to check him over from time to time while he recovers.'

'Thank you for the warning. We'll take great care of him.'

'I'm sure you will.' He smiled at me. 'He's missed you, that's obvious!'

'And we've missed him. I know one little girl who's going to be very happy tonight.'

Caroline. I purred with joy at the thought of seeing her. But there was still another ordeal to face yet: the long car journey back to Little Broomford.

In some ways the journey wasn't quite as bad as the previous one, at the start of the holiday, because at least we didn't have Jessica in the car mewing her head off, keeping me awake. It seemed so long now since that day, and strange to think that back then I'd still had no idea really what to expect from a holiday. Remembering that now, I realised again how much I'd grown up over the course of this summer. For one thing, up till then I'd never been away from my home village before, whereas now I was a well-travelled little cat with a wealth of experience. I'd seen the sea, and had eventually got quite used to it during my time with the feral gang. I'd had my first proper fight, lived to tell the tale and had got some sore places to prove it, and hoped I'd never have to fight like that again. I'd made new friends, learning to get along with cats who were quite frankly not the type we normally fraternise with. Most importantly, I'd learnt to survive. And after all that, the most important thing I'd learnt was that I loved my life with my human family and never wanted to leave them again.

Julian called out to me occasionally as he drove the car home. *Are you all right, there, Charlie?* And *Not too far now, boy.* But most of the time, we were nice and quiet, apart from the music he'd got playing very gently to take my mind off the car's growling and rumbling noises. I was actually asleep again when the car finally stopped outside our house. I woke up at the sound of the car door being pulled open and the voice I loved most in the whole world squealing:

'Charlie! Oh, Charlie, you're home!'

I was so excited to see Caroline's face looking back at me, I jumped up and hit my head on the lid of the silly carrying basket. I meowed so loudly I couldn't even hear what else she was saying, but as she carried my basket into the house, I realised she was crying.

'Don't cry, darling!' Julian said as he followed us in. 'We've got him back now!'

'I know!' she sobbed. 'I'm crying because I'm so happy!'

That was a new one on me. Humans are very odd sometimes! But I didn't care, Caroline could be as odd as she liked, just as long as I could jump into her arms, which I did as soon as she let me out of the basket. We sat on the sofa and I snuggled into her for a lovely long cuddle, purring fit to burst. It was probably the happiest moment of my life.

'He's so thin!' she was saying to her father. 'And what's happened to his eye?'

'He's been in a fight or two, we think,' Julian explained, as Laura came and sat next to Caroline, stroking me and inspecting me carefully. 'He's had a bad bite to his leg there, too – see? It hasn't healed properly so it's left a nasty sore. We've got to take him to our vet tomorrow or the next day, when he's settled down. And the vet in Mudditon thinks he got clawed in his eye – that's what caused the problem there, but we've got drops for him. He's lucky he didn't lose the sight in it.'

'He's got scabby places on his head, too,' Laura said. 'And his poor coat! It's all dull and matted.'

Caroline started to cry again. 'Poor Charlie! It's all my fault!'

'We'll soon nurse him back to health, Caroline,' Laura said gently, putting an arm around her. 'He's young – he'll mend. Just as you will,' she added quietly, looking like she might cry herself.

I looked up at Laura in surprise. What did she mean by that? Was Caroline still not mended? Hadn't they been able to fix her head at the hospital? All my worries about her while we'd been apart immediately came flooding back.

'If Grace and I hadn't been so stupid . . .' she was saying, wiping her eyes.

'What's done is done,' Julian said. 'We've talked about this, haven't we? Losing Charlie was more than enough punishment for you, to say nothing of you getting hurt yourself. I know Grace's parents grounded her for the rest of the holiday, just as we did with you, but you've both learned your lessons, haven't you?'

'Yes,' she whispered. 'Oh, Charlie, I'm so sorry you got lost! I didn't mean for you to run out of the house. It was dark . . . we didn't see you . . . we were being so stupid.'

'It's all right,' I meowed. 'I'm home now, with you. That's all that matters.'

Actually it wasn't. What mattered even more was for me to find out whether she was feeling better. There wasn't any blood dripping from her head anymore, and her finger wasn't looking sore, but what about that horrible illness? Had it come back? Was that what Laura meant? I meowed to myself anxiously, but Caroline just carried on stroking me.

'I'm still absolutely sure it was him, watching me being put into that ambulance, you know,' she said to Laura.

'Well, there must be lots of other little tabby cats just like him. We'll never know for sure.'

'It *was* me!' I told them in Cat, but of course, none of them understood. 'I ran to get help for Caroline! I got the woman from the beach café to come to her rescue!'

'I bet he would've helped us, if he could,' Caroline said. 'I bet that was why he ran out after us – to try to look after us.'

'Yes!' I squeaked. 'Why else would I have done it?'

'Nice idea,' Julian said, smiling at her. 'And if he could, I'm sure he would have done, darling. He loves you very much, that's obvious. But at the end of the day, he's just a little kitten, isn't he. Dogs have certainly been known to look after people, but I've never heard of cats doing it.'

'But he *did* help a human, Daddy! He helped that old lady with the ice cream, when he jumped up at the seagull, didn't he? That's what got into the paper and onto the TV News, wasn't it, and how those ladies came to think it might be him. Everyone in Mudditon thought he was a hero!'

And she cuddled me closer again, wiping her eyes.

'My little hero, Charlie!' she said.

I saw Julian and Laura looking at each other.

'Well,' Julian said. 'Yes, we *think* it was Charlie. And the publicity certainly helped to get him found and brought back, so that's all good. But we can't ever be completely sure. As Laura says, there are lots of little tabby cats around, and—'

'But it *was* him, Daddy. I knew it as soon as we saw him on the TV.'

They didn't argue with her. Nor did I. I just purred in her ear, happy to be called her hero! But despite my worries about Caroline, I must say I was quite interested to hear this conversation. Because although I still didn't understand it at all, it did at least prove I wasn't dreaming when I saw myself in the newspaper and inside the television!

That first day I was home, I didn't even see baby Jessica – she'd already gone to bed. Because of our long journey back from Mudditon, dinner was late and it was getting dark by the time they'd finished eating. Caroline was sent off to bed too then, as she had school the next day, but not before she'd given me another long hug and told me again how much she'd missed me and how much she loved me. I was hoping they were all going to keep up this extra love and attention, and not stop making a fuss of me once they'd got used to me being home again. I followed her upstairs to her room and, to my surprise, before she got ready for bed she picked up a phone from her bedside table.

'Yes, it's mine, Charlie,' she said, waving it at me. 'Daddy and Laura changed their minds! Cool, isn't it!'

It was surprising, that's what it was. I'd heard them with my very own ears, several times, saying she was too young and didn't need one. Perhaps I'd been away so long, she was now old enough. That was a scary thought. But I sat on her bed and listened as she started speaking into it.

'Hi Grace! Guess what – we've got Charlie back!'

I could hear Grace's voice coming out of the phone, squealing with excitement. I have no idea how she got inside it.

'Yes, Daddy brought him home today. We don't know where he's been all this time, but he's been in a fight, and he's skinny and he's got a sore leg and a sore eye, but Laura says we can feed him back to health.'

It was lovely to hear Caroline chatting to her friend, sounding giggly and happy, making me think perhaps there wasn't anything wrong with her anymore after all. But towards the end of her conversation, Grace must have asked her something about how she was feeling, because she sighed and said, 'Oh, you know. The same. Just … tired, still, really, all the time.' She looked at me, smiled and added, 'But it's cheered me up so much, having Charlie back.' And then Laura called up to her to remind her to get herself to bed, and I scampered back downstairs to get some cuddles in with Julian and Laura before it was night-time. But even with all the extra attention, it was hard to forget my worries.

In the morning, I woke up to a strange sound. It was a kind of laughing noise, but a gurgling and bubbling laugh, like a kitten might make, if only we could. I padded into the lounge, and there on the rug was baby Jessica, lying on her back with all her paws waving in the air, while Caroline, dressed in a very smart dark blue outfit with her hair neatly tied up, was tickling her tummy and making her … yes! She was making her laugh! I stopped in the doorway and stared in amazement. Up till then, I'd thought little human kittens like Jessica were only capable of one sound: that awful constant mewing. But there she was, grinning all over her face and bubbling with laughter, and Caroline was smiling at her as if she loved her *almost* as much as she loved me.

'Look, Jessica!' she said, catching sight of me standing there. 'Charlie's back! Charlie's come to say hello to you!'

I trotted a bit closer, wondering whether at any moment Laura would come rushing in to shoo me away from the baby. But Caroline picked me up and sat me on her lap so that Jessica could see me.

'Here he is!' she said. 'Look, Jessica! Pussy cat!'

And she took hold of Jessica's tiny paw and stroked me with it. At first the baby blinked with surprise, but then she started to smile and make the gurgling noise again.

'Ah, she loves you, Charlie,' Caroline said, hugging me. 'Not as much as I do, of course, but nobody ever could.'

'And nobody could love *you* like I do, either,' I meowed to her, rubbing my head against her arm. 'But I'm worried about you. Are you ill again? Why did you say you're so tired? What happened at the hospital?'

'I've got to go to school now, Charlie,' she said, instead of answering me. 'Please promise me you won't ever go wandering off again. I couldn't bear it.'

'I won't if *you* won't,' I said.

And I spent the rest of the day – in between sleeping in my comfortable bed, and eating my delicious food – pondering on the fact that this was what I'd longed for and dreamed of, all the time I was lost. I was home now, I was safe, I was back with my lovely family and I'd never leave them again. But I still couldn't feel completely happy until I found out whether Caroline was all right. And nobody seemed to be telling me.

CHAPTER
SEVENTEEN

Things definitely seemed to have changed at home while I'd been away, and there was still quite a lot that I didn't understand. For instance, why was Caroline dressed in those smart blue clothes and going off to school carrying a huge bag of books? Why was everyone being so nice to each other? I was pleased about this, of course, but it was so different from the way they'd been behaving before the holiday, with all the arguments and slamming of bedroom doors. I did wonder whether it was all because of me – the excitement of having me back home – but nice though that idea was, I had a feeling there was more to it. I was frightened that Julian and Laura were being extra kind to Caroline because they'd found out she was ill again. Caroline was behaving better too – less cross and grumpy, although when she came home from school every day she looked so pale and tired I could hardly bear to think about it.

From time to time, I was also still puzzling over the incident where I saw myself in the television in that shop window. When my family turned their television on in the evening, I tried to climb up to it, or sit on the shelf above it to stare down at it, trying to work out how to get inside it, but there was no way in. It just didn't make sense. But at least I seemed to be making Caroline laugh, even while she was lying on the sofa with that pale face and those dark circles under her eyes that frightened me so much.

Despite my worries, I can't deny I was enjoying getting used to my home comforts again. Having had to grow up quickly, as I've already said, in order to survive my time of living rough, all I wanted to do now was revert to my kittenhood. Safe in the knowledge that nobody was going to throw things at me, jump on me and try to kill me, or swoop down from the sky and peck me to death, I could go back to playing outside in the sunshine. As far as my sore leg would let me, I could enjoy games like chasing leaves that fluttered down from the trees in the wind, jumping out at birds from behind bushes and leaping in the air just for the fun of it. Indoors, I was enjoying playing my old games like peek-a-boo with Caroline from inside an empty cardboard box, and chasing a wind-up toy mouse across the carpet, making both her and Jessica squeal with laughter. Then I would stretch out to rest on my favourite windowsill in the warmth of the sun, or curl up on the sofa cushions in the evening, dreaming happy dreams again.

On my second day back home, Caroline brought Grace to see me after school.

'Oh!' she said, her lower lip wobbling when she looked at me. 'Poor Charlie!'

'He's getting better, though,' Caroline said, picking me up and stroking me. 'Daddy says we've got to keep feeding him lots of good food and milk, and brushing him so that his fur comes through nice and soft again.'

'And will his eye get better? And his poor leg?'

'Yes. We're putting drops in his eye. And Laura's taking him to the vet's tomorrow to make his leg better.'

I flinched slightly at the mention of the vet. But my leg was still painful, so if he could make it better, I knew I had to be brave about it. As for the eye drops, it was horrible having them dripped into my eye, making me shake my head and bat my eye with my paw afterwards. But I knew Julian and Laura wouldn't do that to me unless it was for my own good. I trusted them. It was a good feeling.

'It's all our fault, isn't it, Caro,' Grace said sadly. 'If we hadn't tried to run away…'

'I know. It all seems so ridiculous now, doesn't it? So *childish*.'

'Especially now we know about my great aunt.'

'Yes. Although you'd think your parents would've *told* you she's an old battle-axe who doesn't even like children!'

'Well, to be fair, I suppose they couldn't have known I'd decide it was a good idea for us to go and live with her. I feel really stupid now. Mum says she only sends us money at Christmas and birthdays to make herself feel better because she wants nothing whatsoever to do with the family. That one time she came to visit us, apparently she was supposed to be staying for a week, but she walked out after one day, because she thought Rose and I were badly behaved and made too much noise. We were only little! Mum and Dad were really cross about it. They said she was miserable and unreasonable and they felt insulted. Can you imagine what she'd have said if we'd actually turned up on her doorstep?'

'God, it would have been awful, wouldn't it? What planet were we both on, down in Mudditon, Grace? I mean, I know I was feeling fed up about Jessica getting all the attention, but now, looking back, I think I was just being a spoilt brat.'

'You seem to like Jessica a lot more now!'

'Well, yes, she's getting more interesting now. She doesn't cry so much, and she's sleeping better at night so Laura isn't so tired and ratty. I suppose it made me feel better when she started smiling at me more, and laughing and making that *ga ga* noise. It's kind of cute.'

'She'll grow up into an annoying younger sister soon enough, just like Rose,' Grace said with a shrug. 'Although I suppose having a sister isn't *all* bad. Rose isn't irritating *all* the time. We always used to get on together really well. I don't know what changed.'

'Perhaps it's all part of this growing-up thing – finding people annoying. Now you and Rose go to different schools, and won't be together so much, maybe you'll get on with her better again.'

'Yes.' Grace smiled at Caroline. 'High school's not so bad, is it? The first week was pretty scary, but it would've been awful if we hadn't been together. I'm so pleased your dad and Laura changed their minds about it.'

'Me too. It was all so last-minute, we didn't even know if they'd still get a place for me at Great Broomford. But when we heard it was OK, Laura didn't even make a fuss about having to get me a different uniform. She said it was worth it, for me to be happy again. And I'm glad you're getting used to it too. It was good you managed to talk to your mum and dad about how frightened you were, before we started.'

'I had to, really, with Dad being so furious with me about the running-away thing. When he sat me down and made me spell out exactly what was wrong with me, it all came out, how they weren't taking me seriously about how scared I was. He said afterwards that they were *mortified*. He said however busy they were, they'd always listen to me if I told them I was seriously worried about anything.'

'Yeah. Dad and Laura have said the same kind of thing. You know, about me being frightened about the leukaemia coming back.' I pricked up my ears, my heart racing, waiting to hear more. Had it come back or not? But she just shrugged and went on: 'Dad said it's always best to talk about your fears openly rather than bottling them up and just getting cross and moody.'

'It's not always easy though, is it, talking to parents?' Grace said, laughing. 'They're … well, they're so *old*!'

'Still, one good thing came out of it all,' Caroline said more cheerfully. 'Our parents gave in about us having phones.'

'Yes. To be fair, Mum and Dad did used to let me use that old one of Mum's, but I never took it anywhere because it was so old-fashioned and embarrassing. Anyway, the battery always went flat after about five minutes. It was just a joke! But now we've both got proper ones—'

'—like everyone else!'

'—they'll always be able to keep in touch with us when we're out. I suppose it's fair enough. We did worry the life out of them, didn't we?'

All through this conversation, they'd been stroking me and playing with me, while I listened carefully, trying to get the gist of it all. It seemed my human kitten and her friend had done some fast growing up recently, just like me. Perhaps their smart new blue clothes were making them feel less like children, and that was why they were now talking almost like proper grown-up humans. Nobody seemed to care that they still hadn't told me what had happened to Caroline since we'd been separated. It was frustrating, but I decided eventually that worrying about it wasn't going to help either me or Caroline. And as it happened I did have other things to think about.

First there was the trip to the vet's to get my leg seen to. I can't deny that, despite my more mature outlook on life and having been proved beyond all doubt not to be a scaredy-cat, I still cowered in the travelling basket mewing in fear when we set off in the car. And the smell of the vet's room brought back terrible memories of my experience at that other vet's. I knew I'd behaved really badly on that occasion. Already, I was finding it hard to believe how furiously I'd fought with the humans who were trying to help me. I supposed I really must have been turning into a feral cat at that point. It wasn't a pleasant thought. This time, although I was frightened, I did try not to bite the vet's fingers or struggle quite so much. Although Caroline couldn't come with us because she was at school, and Julian was at work, it was at least reassuring to have Laura there, stroking me and saying calming things to me, while baby Jessica sat in the corner in her car seat waving her paws at me.

'It's all right, Charlie,' the vet said, holding me gently. 'This won't take too long.'

It felt plenty long enough to me. He kept poking around on my sore leg, making me jump and growl, and kept up a running commentary to Laura and his nurse, saying things like *Just clipping his fur back* and *Here we go* and *Right, just cleaning it up again now.* I was glad when he finally announced *OK, I think that's going to heal nicely now, Charlie boy.*

But that wasn't the worst of it. Before he allowed Laura to take me home, he took hold of me and fastened something round my neck. I shook my head from side to side, trying to get rid of it, but it was stuck tight.

'What is it?' I meowed crossly at Laura, but to my annoyance she was laughing at me.

'Oh, look at him!' she said. 'Poor Charlie, he's not going to like that one bit!'

'I know. But it's important that he doesn't lick that wound,' the vet said. 'We don't want any more infection. Keep it on for a week, and keep him inside. Then bring him back to see me – I'd like to check on him anyway – then we should be able to dispense with it.'

What on earth was it? I spent the whole journey back home tossing my head from side to side, knocking the thing against the edges of the basket.

'Suffering codfish!' I shouted at Laura as she carried me in from the car. 'What in the name of bloody catnip…?'

I stopped, growling to myself unhappily. I really didn't want to revert to the kind of language I'd picked up during my homeless period. But honestly, this was unbelievable!

What were they doing to me? Hadn't I been through enough? And when I saw the cat flap being locked before Laura had even taken me out of the basket, I yowled at her crossly. Even though I'd seen it locked with my own eyes, I went straight up to it to butt it with my head in protest, but the huge thing round my neck got in the way. Even if I'd been allowed out, I wouldn't have been able to get through my flap. It was ridiculous! How was I supposed to live like this?

'Oh dear,' Laura said. 'You'll get used to it, Charlie. It's only for a little while.'

Huh. I went to lie down in my bed and have a sulk, but have you ever tried lying down with a gigantic collar around your neck? And there was worse to come. Later on when Laura put my dinner down on the floor, I had to lean right over the dish, so that the collar was touching the floor all the way round it. I felt like I was cut off from the rest of the world while I was eating. Caroline came home from school just as I finished my meal, and she gasped with surprise when she saw me.

'Oh! What's Charlie got that thing on for?'

'It's to stop him trying to lick his wound. And he's not allowed outside till I take him back to the vet's next week.'

'Ah, he won't like that, will he?'

'No. So we're back to being careful about open doors, Caroline.' Laura gave her a look, which I understood only too well.

'OK. I'll be careful, I promise,' Caroline said. They both stood for a while, watching me as I tried unsuccessfully to wash myself after my meal.

'I can't even have a wash!' I meowed crossly, shaking my head so that the stupid thing knocked against the kitchen units. 'Do you want me to get even muckier than I was when I was living rough?'

'And we'll need to groom him,' Laura told Caroline. 'He can't do it for himself while he's in the collar. And the vet said that it's best not to take it off, at all. He'll get used to it more quickly if he wears it all the time.'

Well, that was just great, wasn't it? I charged around the house angrily for a bit, trying to shake the thing off, but of course all I succeeded in doing was knocking everything over and falling over twice myself.

'Charlie, calm down, you're not helping matters!' Caroline said, giggling. She bent down to pick me up. 'You do look funny.'

I couldn't believe it! I'd have thought I could rely on Caroline, at least, to be sympathetic, but it seemed I'd just become a figure of fun. But she was right, of course. By the next day I'd adapted to the collar and eventually even gave in with a good grace to the fact that I was locked indoors. And who did I have to thank for my acceptance of the situation? Well, the same sensible older cat who'd given me the benefit of his advice and experience all my life. Yes, my friend Oliver, of course.

CHAPTER
EIGHTEEN

I'll tell everyone what happened, shall I, Ollie? Unless you want to take over? No? Oh, you think I'm doing a good job of telling my story, for a little kitten who's never done any public meowing before? Well, that's very kind, thank you. I learned from the best! Although I keep reminding you, I'm not a little kitten anymore. Look at me. I'm fully grown, and you must admit now you're hearing my story, I've got even more experience of life now than you have. But I suppose, to you, I'll always be *little kitten*, won't I?

Well, everyone, as you know, Oliver has always taken a special interest in me and looked after me. I know I have a real father, but tell me – where is he, eh? Where's old Tabby when I'm telling my story to the rest of the village cats? Exactly! He's never around. He's probably off somewhere chasing some young female. I don't mind; that's just the way he is, and it was nice that Oliver took on the role of mentoring me, and my sisters here, instead. I've always looked up to him as an example of how to be a good cat. So when I disappeared, naturally Ollie was worried. Apparently he kept on coming to the Big House, looking for me, meowing around the outside of the house, but at first, of course, nobody was there because we were all at our holiday home in Mudditon. And then, apparently, one day he turned up at the house and found that the rest of the family were back home, but not me. He was more worried than ever then.

One day Caroline heard him meowing outside, and let him in. As you know, my family love Oliver – almost, but not quite, as much as they love me. He's told me that Caroline was crying as she stroked him, saying I'd got lost and it was all her fault. Ollie was very upset to hear this, and apparently he went back to the Big House several times after that, to see whether I'd returned.

That day, after my first uncomfortable night's sleep wearing the horrible collar, I was eating my breakfast and having a moan to myself at the same time about the awkwardness of eating with that thing on, when I heard a familiar meow outside the kitchen door. I left my food for a minute and trotted over to look through the cat flap, and I nearly fell over with excitement. Ollie was outside, calling to me through the flap. I can't tell you how pleased I was to see him, and I think he was even more excited to see me because he proceeded to shout at the top of his voice and paw at the locked flap.

'What on earth's going on?' Laura said, coming into the kitchen, because I was now making almost as much noise as Ollie was, and pawing at the cat flap from inside too. 'Oh!' she said. 'Hello, Oliver! I suppose you want to come in and play with your friend now he's back. Hang on a minute and I'll let you in.'

With which she picked me up and held on to me while she unlocked the flap. As Ollie jumped through, she put me back down and I was so excited, I ran around the room madly, knocking into two chairs and the side of the fridge with the stupid collar.

'You're back,' he meowed at me. 'I've been looking for you everywhere.'

'I know, I've been lost, and living rough, and – oh my tail and whiskers, it's so good to see you! I've got so much to tell you about.'

'So it seems.' He stared at me. 'I'd like to rub faces with you, but what you're wearing makes that a tad difficult. And I have to say, you're not looking too good. You've lost weight, haven't you? And what's happened to your eye?'

'It's a long story. But first, can you tell me how I can get this dratted thing off? It's driving me mad. I keep bashing into things, and they won't let me go outside. Maybe if you could chew the edge, there, or get your claw in between the collar and my neck...?'

Oliver looked at me seriously for a moment.

'Did the vet put it on you? Have you had some kind of operation done?'

'Well, yes, he did something to my bad leg, see? It's still a bit sore but I think it's getting better now.'

'Exactly, Charlie. It's getting better because of whatever the vet did, and they only make us wear those collars to help us get better. So you need to keep it on.'

'Whose side are you on?' I said sulkily. 'I thought I could rely on you to help me.'

'No. You can rely on me to tell you what you need to know. Don't you trust your humans anymore? Was it their fault you got lost, or what?'

'No. It was ... well, it was partly Caroline's fault, I suppose, but I don't blame her, she's still only a kitten really and she made a bad mistake. I suppose I *did* forget how to trust humans, for a while, but now I'm back home, of course I do trust my family.'

'So stop fighting against them, Charlie! They're only making you wear the collar, and keeping you indoors, until you get better. And looking at you, quite frankly you do need a period of convalescence. I hate to think what you've been through.'

'Just you wait till I tell you all about it,' I said. Then I sighed. 'But I suppose you're right, I'll just have to give in and put up with this till they say it can come off.'

'That's my boy. Be sensible. Now, finish your breakfast and then I'll give your face a wash, shall I, as it doesn't look as if you can do it yourself.'

'Thanks, Ollie. It's so good to be back with you. Afterwards we can lie in that sunny corner of the lounge together while I tell you my story.'

'Charlie, I'd love to, but if it's a long story it's going to have to wait till another day. I've got to go and visit Nicky today.'

'Nicky?' I lifted my head from my food bowl to look at him as well as I could round the edge of the collar.

'Yes. I'm really worried about her. Not quite as worried as I was about you, of course, but now that I know you're back, and safe, I want to try and help her. If only I could work out how.'

It was so typical of Oliver. He's spent half his life helping the humans in the village. No wonder they all think he's a special kind of cat.

230

'What's happened to her?' I asked him. As you know, I'm very fond of Nicky myself, so I didn't like to think of her being in some kind of trouble.

'She's just so unhappy these days. And it's all her stupid male's fault.'

'Daniel? Why? What's he done?' I had a sudden memory of Nicky and Laura chatting on the sofa of our holiday home. 'Oh, is it something to do with him going to the pub? Nicky mentioned that when she came to Mudditon. I suppose as you live at the pub, you must see him in there?'

'Yes, I see him every single night! And he doesn't just have one quick drink of beer and then go home. He's there for ages. I pop in to see Nicky most days, and quite often she's crying, Charlie, because he's leaving her on her own all the time with their human kitten and she's told me she thinks he doesn't want to be with her anymore. It'd be different if she were a cat, wouldn't it. Our females expect to be left with the kittens while their males go off hunting and ... um, well...'

'... and philandering. I know all about it, Ollie. You don't need to be coy with me. I'm grown up now, I keep telling you, and I might be neutered, like you, but I've been living with some guys who spent most of their lives talking about either stealing food or mating with females.'

'Really?' He looked a bit shocked.

'Yes. Let me tell you—'

'I do want to hear all about it, Charlie, but at the minute I can't think straight for worrying about Nicky. I seem to be the only one who can cheer her up.'

'Oh, all right then.' I felt a bit let down. What about cheering me up? I had a bad leg and a bad eye and wasn't allowed out, after all. 'Go off and cheer her up. Don't worry about me.'

'Don't be like that. I'll come back, all right? I promise. Meanwhile *you* promise *me* you'll be a sensible kitt ... sorry, *cat* ... and stop complaining about wearing that collar and staying indoors. I want you to get better.'

So we both kept our promises. I settled down, accepted that my life was going to be severely restricted until the vet allowed me back my freedom, and tried to be patient. And Oliver duly came back to see me again the next day.

'So what's the news with Nicky?' I asked, but he just shook his head sadly and said there was no change.

'I keep hanging around Daniel every evening in the pub, meowing at him, trying to persuade him he ought to go home, but he's so stupid when he starts drinking beer, he just thinks I'm being friendly. I'm going to have a word with Tabby. He's helped me in the past when I've wanted some support with a difficult human. He sometimes needs a bit of persuasion, though!'

'Good luck with that, then,' I said, knowing what my father's like. And as I expected, the next couple of times Oliver came back to see me, it was to report that he'd had no luck finding him.

'Probably taken himself off somewhere for a few days,' I said. 'He'll be back eventually.'

'I know. I'm not worried about him – Tabby can look after himself. I was just hoping he could help me think of a way to do something about Daniel.'

I sat up, suddenly excited. So excited, I forgot about my collar for a minute and nearly knocked Ollie over with it.

'Never mind about him,' I meowed, '*I'll* help you.'

'You?' Oliver looked startled. 'But you're only—'

'Don't you dare say I'm only a little kitten. If you'd only let me tell you what I've been through recently...'

'I'm sorry, Charlie. I realise you're dying to tell me your story, and I haven't been very good company, have I? You know how I worry about my favourite humans.'

'Yes, I do. But I'm trying to tell you, I've become a very brave and very resourceful cat since I went away. And, well, you've done such a lot to help *me*, when I was growing up, I think it's time you let me help you, for once, instead of trying to rely on my unreliable father.'

Oliver purred at me thoughtfully.

'That's all very well, and I appreciate the offer. But for one thing you're not allowed out. And even if you were, you wouldn't be much use in a crisis while you've got that thing stuck on your neck.'

'So wait a few more days, can't you, for mewing out loud? What's the rush? If he's in the pub every single evening...?'

'I suppose you're right.' He got up and flicked his tail anxiously. 'I just hate seeing Nicky so upset.' Then he glanced back at me and added, 'And to be honest, I'm having a hard job thinking of you as a grown-up cat. You're still not looking all that well, either. Are you sure you'd be up for whatever it is we have to do?'

For the love of catnip! Over the course of the summer, I'd been lost in a strange town, rescued two human kittens from an accident on the beach, been violently attacked by feral cats, persuaded their leader not only to submit to me but to adopt me into their gang, learned to survive by scavenging and sleeping rough, and saved an old lady from vicious seagulls. And Oliver was asking if I thought I could manage a little bit of persuasion of a friendly human?

'I think I can cope,' I said, trying to toss my head at him but once again getting unbalanced by the stupid collar.

'Well, I guess I need to start accepting that you're not such a little kitten anymore,' he said. 'OK. I don't suppose it'll be long now till they take you back to the vet, so let's say that as soon as they let you outside again, you come and meow for me at the pub after dark. Daniel's bound to be there. You'll have to follow me and do what I tell you.'

'Fine,' I said, feeling a bit patronised, as you can imagine. 'But when you hear what I've been up to—'

'Yes, I know, I know – I'll hear all about it, Charlie, don't worry, just as soon as we've sorted out this problem, all right?'

And with that, he meowed for Laura to let him out again, and with a wave of his tail, he was gone.

CHAPTER
NINETEEN

When the day finally came for the vet to take the collar off me, I nearly jumped off his table with joy. I felt light and free and frisky as a ... well, frisky as a little kitten, I suppose.

'He certainly seems to have cheered up a lot since last week,' the vet said, and Laura laughed.

'He hasn't been very happy about being kept indoors. It's just lucky his friend Oliver has been visiting, to keep him company.'

'Oliver, the pub cat? He's a very unusual cat, that one, isn't he? Seems to understand humans, somehow – and befriending another cat, too? That's unusual in itself.'

'No it isn't!' I meowed at him. 'You humans just *think* it's unusual because *you* don't understand *us*. We often make friends with other cats actually.'

But, of course, even vets don't bother to learn Cat, do they, although you'd have thought it should be part of the job. So he completely ignored me, and busied himself instead with checking my leg and my eye, and putting a nasty, cold hard object into a very personal part of my body to take my temperature.

'Well, I'm pleased to say that he's on the mend,' he said eventually. 'The leg's healed well, his eye has cleared up, and he seems to be putting some weight back on. He should be fine to go outside again now and get back to normal. Just bring him back in if you're at all worried, won't you.'

'Of course. Thank you.'

'I'm just glad it's been a happy ending for the little fellow,' he said, giving me a stroke. 'Hard to imagine how he survived while he was missing, but I reckon he lost a few of his nine lives in the process.'

'No, I didn't!' I protested. I'm pretty sure I would have known about it if I had!

'Come on then, Charlie,' said Laura, picking me up and putting me in the horrible basket to drive me home. 'You can go off and play with Oliver now, to your heart's content.'

Play? We had business to attend to! But of course, in the meantime, I was certainly looking forward to a run around outside. I'd noticed from the kitchen window that there was quite a layer of fallen leaves now on my lawn, and I was itching to get out there and dance around in them. I really wanted Caroline to come outside and play with me, but as usual, after school she was too tired to do much apart from lying on the sofa. I hadn't told Ollie yet of my worries about her, but I knew he loved her too. At the moment he was far too concerned about Nicky to think of anything else, but I decided that as soon as I'd helped him with that situation, I'd ask his advice about Caroline.

After my dinner that evening, I trotted off down the lane into the village, as arranged, to meet Oliver at the pub where he lives. I jumped up onto the windowsill, pleased to find my injured leg was working so much better now, and meowed through the glass until he saw me.

'Is Daniel in there?' I asked when Oliver appeared from his cat flap in the back yard.

'Yes, as usual. Thanks for coming. You look more normal now.'

'I should hope so, without that thing round my neck. So what are we going to do? Leap on his lap and yowl in his ear till he goes home?'

He stared at me. 'That's a bit aggressive, isn't it?'

I blinked. Was it?

'Not where I've come from,' I said, thinking back to some of the tactics the feral boys used.

'Charlie, wherever you've been recently, please remember you're back in polite cat society now,' he admonished me. 'We don't go in for jumping on humans and yowling at them, around here – not unless they've hurt us, of course.'

'No, all right, fair enough,' I said, duly chastised. 'So, what do you say we should do? Sing to him? Blink him kisses?'

'No need for sarcasm, either. I thought perhaps we should bring Nicky to the pub and let him see how upset she is.'

'How's that going to work? She'll be looking after her human kitten, Benjamin.'

'I know. She can bring him with her. When he sees her with the baby he'll remember his responsibilities and feel ashamed of himself.'

I didn't want to argue with Oliver, but it sounded pretty unlikely to me. For a start, I wasn't convinced we'd be able to persuade Nicky to bring the baby out to the pub at night, and even if she did, I suspected Daniel wouldn't be impressed.

'What's wrong?' Oliver said, as I hadn't replied. 'Are you not up for it after all?'

'Of course I am. Come on then, let's give it a go,' I said.

I followed him down the road to Nicky and Daniel's house, and once again I showed off the strength of my newly healed leg by jumping up onto the nearest window-sill. Oliver jumped up beside me and we put our noses up against the cold glass.

'She's there, sitting on the sofa,' Oliver said. 'Come on, let's make a noise and get her to let us in.'

'Hang on, who's that?' I said. A tall, thin male with lots of facial fur was sitting next to Nicky on the sofa. 'Is it her father?'

'No, I don't think so. I think it's the male who lives next door. Put your ear against the glass, Charlie,' Oliver said, doing the same himself. 'Let's try to hear what they're saying.'

In fact I could only hear the male's voice at first. Nicky didn't seem to be saying a lot.

'I prefer Thai food myself,' he was saying. He had a peculiar kind of smile on his face, and he seemed to be leaning too close to Nicky. She didn't look very comfortable and was edging further along the sofa. 'I know a nice little Thai restaurant in town. The food is delicious, and it's a really nice atmosphere in there. Do you like Thai? I think you'd enjoy it. Maybe I could take you there one of these evenings when you're all on your own.'

Nicky gave a funny little laugh that didn't sound quite right. 'I've got Benjamin asleep upstairs, remember.'

'Can't you get a babysitter? We wouldn't have to be out late. I'd drive you.'

'No, Kevin, I can't. It wouldn't be right.'

'So is it right that he spends every evening at the pub? You've already told me you're fed up with being left on your own.'

'I shouldn't have said that.'

'You wouldn't have said it if you didn't mean it. I'm glad you felt you could confide in me, Nicky. Glad to be here for you, as a friend, you know, someone you can talk to. You obviously need that, and God knows you deserve it. You work so hard, looking after Benjamin all on your own, as well as minding other people's children.'

'It's my job. It's what I do. Dan works hard too.'

'Yes, but he's not being fair to you, is he? You deserve to have a bit of fun in your life too. You need someone to take you out, treat you a bit special and show you some attention. Everyone needs that, don't they?'

He reached out a paw to take hold of one of hers, but she moved it away, staring straight ahead of her, going a bit red in the face.

'Don't, Kevin,' she said. 'I ... look, I'll go and make us both a cup of tea, shall I?'

She got up, but as she did he reached out for her paw again, giving it a little stroke.

'I'm not here to upset you in any way, Nicky. I'm just trying to be a friend to you.'

'I know, and I appreciate it.' She shifted from one back paw to the other, still looking uncomfortable. 'So: tea or coffee?'

'I've heard enough,' Oliver said, jumping down from the windowsill. 'It's bad, Charlie, very bad. Worse than I thought. They're on the verge of mating, I'm afraid. It's the same as what happens with unneutered cats when they're getting randy.'

'Really?' It was nothing whatever like the kind of mating I'd witnessed among my feral cat friends. There was no long drawn-out meowing and paw brushing involved in that, unfortunately, although I think their females might have liked it a bit better if there had been.

'Yes. I can't expect a little kitt—cat … like you to under-stand such things, but I can assure you we need to move fast.'

'What are we going to do, then? Rush in and jump him? Go for his throat?'

He gasped. 'Charlie, what in the name of all that's warm and cosy has come over you since you went missing? We don't *go for the throat* of a human, even if we don't like what they're doing.'

'Sorry. I keep forgetting myself.'

'Yes, well, the sooner you remember yourself the better. No, what we're going to do is go back to the pub and persuade Daniel to come straight home, right this minute, before it's too late.'

'How are we going to do that? Jump on…?' I stopped quickly, seeing the look he was giving me. 'Whisper in his ear?' I tried instead.

'We have to walk backwards and forwards to and from the pub door,' Oliver said, as we started to run back down the road. 'Watch me, and do what I do, OK? I taught Daniel to understand a bit of Cat body language when there were some important issues last year. It'll soon come back to him. As long as he hasn't had too many of those drinks of beer. It seems to make humans extremely forgetful.'

In no time at all, we were jumping through the cat flap into the back room of the pub.

'Follow me,' Oliver said, striding ahead of me into the main room where everyone seemed to be talking very loudly or laughing and lifting their glasses of drink to their mouths. 'There he is, by the window. Now remember, watch me and do what I do.'

'OK.' I followed him to where Daniel was sitting with a couple of other males. They had drinks on the table in front of them and were deep in conversation.

'I still say West Ham should've been allowed that goal,' one of the other males said.

'Don't talk rubbish, man,' Daniel said, laughing. Then he glanced down and said, 'Oh, there you are, Ollie. And who's this you've brought home with you? It's little Charlie Kitten, isn't it?'

'I'm *not* a little kitten now!' I meowed crossly, but Oliver gave me a look and hissed:

'Stay focused on the job, Charlie!'

'We heard he'd been found. He looks a bit skinny, doesn't he?' one of Daniel's friends said, bending down to stroke me.

243

I could sense that Oliver was getting frustrated.

'Never mind about all that!' he meowed. 'Daniel needs to come with us.' And he proceeded to stalk across to the main door of the pub, his tail waving in the air. 'Come on!'

I copied him, meowing as I went, waving my tail.

'What's up with them?' the other friend asked. 'Do they want to go out? George!' he called across to Ollie's owner, who ran the pub. 'What's up with your cat? Has he been fed?'

'Oh, for mewing out loud!' Oliver said to me. 'They're so slow to catch on. Come on, do it again.'

We turned round, ran back to Daniel's table, meowing loudly, and once again walked towards the door, looking back at him. Suddenly, he put down his glass, staring at us.

'I think they want me to go with them,' he said.

'What? Are you serious? Did they talk to you, or what?' one of the others laughed.

'In a way, yes. Oliver's done it before. He has ... some kind of strange powers.' Ignoring the sniggers from his friends, he pushed back his chair and got up. 'It might be an emergency,' he said, suddenly looking a bit frightened. He threw some money down on the table. 'Sorry, lads – got to go.'

'See?' Oliver meowed to me as he opened the pub door and we all ran out into the night. 'I told you we could do it.'

'Yes. Well done.' We started to run, ahead of Daniel, leading him back along the road to his own house.

'What is it, boys?' he panted, running after us. 'It's not ... not Nicky, is it? Oh my God, please don't let it be something wrong with Benjamin? God, no, please, don't

244

let anything have happened to them, while I was...' He broke off, and when I looked round I saw him wiping his face with his paw. In the light of the street lamps he looked white and scared. 'What the hell have I been doing?' he muttered. 'I'll never forgive myself if...'

But he didn't get any further, because by now we were at his front door and he'd already got his key in his paw. He opened the door and was just about to charge in, when we all heard the sound of voices coming from the lounge. I glanced at Oliver. Kevin with the furry face was obviously still here. Daniel froze where he was on the doorstep, listening.

'But why not?' Kevin was saying in a soft, wheedling kind of voice. 'We're getting along so well together, aren't we? And let's face it, your marriage is ... well, it's pretty much on the rocks, isn't it? You can't deny...'

I heard Daniel gasp. He took a couple of steps into the hallway, but stopped dead again as we heard Nicky interrupting Kevin. This time her voice was a lot louder than before, and a lot crosser.

'That's enough, Kevin! I think you'd better go.'

'Oh, come on, Nicky! You know you want to...'

'No, I don't! I don't know how I've given you the impression that I was interested in you in that way, but if I have, I'm very sorry. I *did* think we got on well, as neighbours, as friends perhaps, and I've enjoyed your company in the evenings. It's true Daniel's been neglecting me recently—'

Daniel gasped again, and put his paw to his head. He looked like he was going to fall over.

'—and yes, it has made me sad, but that doesn't mean I've stopped loving him. And it doesn't mean I'm going to jump into the arms of another man, just because you've told me about your divorce, and let me confide in you. I shouldn't have done that. Daniel and I will sort out our problems. I don't want you to come round anymore.'

'Oh, surely there's no need to be like that,' he said. 'I think—'

But we never found out what he thought. Because at that point Daniel suddenly seemed to burst into life again and, throwing his keys on the hall table, he raced into the lounge and skidded to a halt within nose-touching distance of furry-faced Kevin, who staggered backwards away from Nicky with a look of surprise.

'You heard my wife,' Daniel said in a growly voice like an angry dog. 'Go.'

'No need for that, mate,' Kevin protested, waving his paws in front of him as if he was smoothing something down. 'Nicky and I have just been having a nice friendly chat over a cup of tea. While you were *neglecting her*. As she said.'

'Dan, I didn't say … well, I didn't mean…' Nicky was saying. 'Don't! Dan, leave him alone. Don't hit him! It was my fault, I must have given him the wrong impression.'

I felt my fur standing on end. Daniel had got hold of Kevin by his jumper and had his paw screwed up into a fist, like a weapon. Kevin's eyes were wide with fear, and he was making a stuttering noise that sounded like 'Uh … uh … uh …'

'Dan!' Nicky squealed more loudly. 'Don't! It won't help! Please don't do something you'll regret.'

'Sparrows alive!' I meowed.

I wasn't going to wait to see what happened. Nicky was one of my favourite humans, and Daniel was making her upset, even more upset than she'd been with Kevin. I wasn't going to stand for it. I wasn't a timid little kitten anymore, I was a fighter, a rescuer, a cat who sorted things out and got things done. Just as Daniel was raising his paw to hit Kevin right in his furry face, I leapt up onto the sofa, threw myself at Daniel and clung to his jacket by my claws, yowling in his ear.

'Stop it, for the love of catnip!' I shouted. 'No fighting! Nicky doesn't like it.'

'Ouch! Bloody hell, Charlie, what the hell are you doing? Get off me, you crazy kitten. For God's sake!' he cried, struggling to loosen my claws from the cloth of his jacket. The fight seemed to have gone out of him, because even though I'd shocked him, he was being gentle with me now. 'There you go. Get down,' he said, putting me back on the floor. 'Stay there! What's the matter, woman?' he added, turning to Nicky, who seemed to be trying not to laugh.

'Sorry.' She reached out and put both paws round his waist. 'He didn't hurt you, did he? I'm sorry, Dan, but that was so funny. It was … as if he knew someone had to stop you. Are you all right?'

'Yes.' Daniel stared back at her. 'I'm OK. I'm sorry. I lost my temper, and you're right, it would only have made things worse.'

'Yes. He's not worth it. He was just trying his luck. I shouldn't have let him get so close to me. It was stupid of me.'

'No. Stupid of *me*, leaving you on your own every night, without giving a thought to how you felt. I'm such an idiot, such a selfish idiot! God, Nicky, if you ever left me I don't know what I'd do.'

'I'm not going to leave you, you fool. I knew we'd sort things out eventually. And I know you're working so hard, I can understand you want a drink with your mates sometimes, but...'

'But not every night. It's not fair, and I shouldn't have been doing it. I should be coming home to you and Benjamin. Can you forgive me?'

'Of course. Don't be daft.'

'And you won't see Kevin anymore?' He turned to look around the room. 'Where is he?'

'He sneaked out quickly when Charlie threw himself at you,' Oliver meowed. Oliver was looking at me in a very strange way. 'I think ... I have to say ... I think you saved the day just then, Charlie boy.'

'I don't think we'll be seeing much of Kevin now,' Nicky said, laughing again. 'You and Charlie have both scared the life out of him.'

'Good. What a creep! I suppose I should feel sorry for him. He's probably lonely, and wishes he had a lovely wife like you to come home to.'

'Yes, well, he'll have to find one of his own.' She cuddled up to him and they started to kiss each other.

'I think we should make ourselves scarce now,' I meowed at Oliver.

'Let those two cats out, will you?' Daniel muttered at the same time.

'Did you bring them home with you?' Nicky asked him as she went to open the door for us.

'Um, well, actually they brought *me* home,' he said. 'I know you think I'm mad, but I'm telling you, Ollie here has some kind of strange powers. He told me there was an emergency.'

'Right.' She giggled. 'Well, if that's the case, I reckon little Charlie has the same powers too. He saved you from your own temper just now.'

'Yeah.' He was watching us both as we trotted to the front door. 'In fact they might well have saved our marriage. Amazing.'

'Job done!' I said to Oliver, and we started to walk home together.

CHAPTER
TWENTY

It must have been late at night by the time we said goodbye outside Oliver's pub. People were coming out of the door, calling out goodnight to each other.

'Closing time,' Ollie said knowledgeably. 'Will you be all right walking home by yourself, Charlie?'

'Of course I will,' I meowed. I was beginning to feel impatient with his fussing over me. 'I've been used to going out at night scavenging for food.'

For a minute he didn't reply, but just looked at me, his head on one side.

'You really *have* got a story to relate, haven't you?' he said eventually.

'Yes! I keep telling you I have.'

'And now we've got Nicky and Daniel sorted out, I'm looking forward to hearing it.'

'Good. I'm looking forward to telling you, too. Come to my place tomorrow?'

'Definitely.' He stared at me again. 'You've certainly changed, Charlie. You *are* more grown up, and more confident, somehow. I couldn't believe the way you stopped Daniel from hitting that Kevin, back there.'

'I'm sorry if it wasn't very … polite behaviour.'

'Nonsense. You're quite right, sometimes a situation calls for quick thinking and bold action rather than politeness. What you did back there saved the day. And you heard

Daniel, we've probably saved their marriage too. Well done, Charlie, my little protégé! I'm proud of you.'

He rubbed his face against mine.

'Thanks, Ollie. But you taught me all I know,' I said.

'That used to be true, but it's not anymore. You've learned a lot more since you've been away. Things I could never have taught you.'

Yes. I knew I'd learned a lot from the feral cats, and I'd never forget them, or the time I spent with them. But I hoped my dear, kind friend Oliver would never need to learn about any of those things. In a funny kind of way, I almost felt more grown up than him now, even though it was me who was always going to be *little kitten*.

The next morning I woke up early, looking forward to finally being able to tell Ollie the whole story of my time in Mudditon. But first I needed to talk to him about Caroline.

'So have they actually said her illness has come back?' he asked, when I brought the subject up as soon as he arrived through the cat flap.

'Not exactly. But when I first came home I heard Laura saying to Caroline that I'd get better *just as she would*. And then Caroline told Grace that the reason she was moody and cross before was that she'd been frightened about being ill again. But apart from that, nobody's saying anything.'

'And is she not being moody and cross anymore?'

'No – well, not most of the time, anyway. But she's really, really tired and her face looks white, and when she comes home from her new school she just lies on the sofa.'

Ollie meowed in distress when he heard this, and walked round and round on the spot for a minute, obviously thinking it over.

'I don't like the sound of that,' he admitted. 'That's how she looked when she was ill before. And has her fur come off her head?'

'No. Well, not yet, anyway. If anything, it's grown longer. She ties it up so it looks like a horse's tail.'

'And she hasn't had to go off to the hospital place?'

'Not as far as I know. Not since we were in Mudditon, anyway – the holiday town. She was in hospital there because … well, that's another story. But nobody's told me what happened while she was there.'

'I don't know what to think, then, Charlie. Perhaps it's the new school that's making her tired? I was outside Grace's house the other day when she came home carrying such a big bag of books, she was almost bent double. I don't know why humans make their kittens carry so many books. Surely they can only look at one at a time?'

'I know, it's weird, isn't it? But what can I do, Ollie – you're the clever one – how can I find out what's wrong with her?'

'I'm afraid you'll just have to keep listening to their conversations. Or you could show Caroline how worried you are about her by jumping on her lap and mewing a lot.'

'I keep trying that. I get lots of cuddles, but no answers.'

'Oh dear.' Poor Oliver looked as worried now as I was. 'Well, the only other thing I can suggest is, I'll make lots of extra visits to Grace and her family, as well as to Nicky and Daniel, and listen carefully to all *their* conversations. If Caroline is ill again, they must be really worried too, and they're bound to talk to each other about it. I'll report back to you as soon as I find anything out, all right?'

With which he turned round and headed back to the cat flap.

'Aren't you staying to hear my story?' I called after him, disappointed.

'No, Charlie, sorry,' he meowed at me. 'Not now you've told me this about Caroline – I won't be able to concentrate until we've found out what's wrong.'

'No, of course not,' I said, feeling guilty now for even suggesting it. How could the story of my time in Mudditon possibly compare in importance with Caroline's health? 'You're quite right. Thanks for your help, Ollie.'

When Caroline came home that afternoon, I spent ages sitting on her lap mewing sadly in her ear. But in the end I had to stop because she called out to Laura that she was worried *I* was ill because I kept crying.

'I'm fine,' I purred at her. 'It's you I'm worried about.'

But she still didn't tell me anything.

The next day must have been a Saturday, as nobody was going to school or work, and I could tell straight away that something was going on with my family. They were all talking at once, excitedly, like there was going to be something different happening. I listened carefully, hoping it wasn't going to be another holiday!

'How did they find out he was back home?' Caroline was saying.

'Well, it was a series of things, really,' Julian said. 'You know I wrote to the two ladies in Mudditon who found him and took him to the vet there?'

They were talking about me! I sat up, listening even more carefully.

'Yes, I know, you said you were letting them know how well he was recovering, and that you'd given their reward money to Cats' Protection because the ladies didn't want to accept it.'

'That's right. Well, coincidentally, it seems it was the niece of one of those two ladies who had put that original video on YouTube—'

'The one of Charlie that was on TV?'

'Yes.' He hesitated. 'Presuming it *was* Charlie, of course.'

'Dad, it definitely was!'

'Yes, it was, Julian,' Laura agreed. 'I was convinced, the moment you brought him back home. He had the same injuries as the cat in the video!'

'Yes, that's true. Well, as you know, when these things are popular on YouTube, they escalate—'

'It's called *going viral*, Dad,' Caroline said. She seemed to know a lot more these days. It must have been because of her new school.

'Right.' Julian and Laura exchanged a smile over the top of Caroline's head. 'Yes, it went viral. Well, it seems people in Mudditon were still interested in what happened to Charlie, because of the bit on TV, and because everyone was saying on social media that he was the same cat who was in the "Missing" posters I put up around the town. When our two ladies got my letter, the niece updated her Facebook and Twitter accounts, telling people Charlie had been brought back home and was making a good recovery. Apparently loads of people were following the story, and commenting on it.'

'Ah. That's nice,' Laura said.

I was pleased, too, to hear people in Mudditon were interested in me, but I just wished my feral cat friends could know I was safe and well. They probably had even less idea than me what Facebook or Twitter were, though. Twitter sounded like something to do with sparrows so I couldn't quite see the relevance.

'Well, because of it all going *viral* again,' Julian went on, 'it got picked up once more by the local paper in Mudditon. They ran a cute story about how the little cat who saved the old lady from the seagull was found and returned safely home.'

'And that's how the BBC's got hold of it again,' Laura finished.

'Yes.' Julian paused. 'Although there's a bit more to it than that, apparently. Something new has come up. The guy who called me said he'll explain when they get here.'

'They're coming here?' Caroline squealed. 'Really?'

'Yes! They're on their way. They've asked if they can talk to us, and take some footage of Charlie at home.'

'We'd better lock the cat flap again!' Laura said, jumping up. 'In case he runs outside and isn't here when they come!'

'Good thinking,' Julian said, although needless to say I didn't agree. Wasn't it bad enough that I'd been locked inside all that time I was wearing the collar? And did they really think I wouldn't come back indoors as soon as these people came – whoever they were – to see me? If I was supposed to be the centre of attention, I was going to want to be here, after all!

'Wow, this is so cool!' Caroline said. 'We're going to be on TV. Can Grace come round?'

'Yes.' Laura smiled at her. 'Of course.'

Caroline rushed off to talk to Grace on her new phone.

'So what do you think the new development is?' Laura asked Julian.

'I really can't imagine.'

'But you're sure this is a good idea – the TV thing? For Caroline?'

'I don't think it'll hurt, do you? They'll want to talk to her, but I've warned the guy on the phone that I don't want her upset. We're not going into the fact that the girls were trying to run away.'

'Good. And I suppose it might be quite educational for her and Grace to see how the filming's done. And a bit of excitement for them too.'

So, you see, Oliver, that was why my cat flap was locked again when you came round to see me. We meowed to each other from either side of the flap, but when Laura saw you, she said, 'Oh dear, sorry, Oliver, I don't think we'd better have you in here today, not with the television people coming round, with their cameras and everything. An extra cat will just add to the confusion.'

And eventually, of course, you gave up and went off, probably wondering if they were keeping me indoors because I was ill again. I wasn't. I was excited, although I wasn't quite sure what I was excited about yet. Grace turned up, and she and Caroline sat in the kitchen with me, talking and giggling together and looking at their watches all the time and wondering how much longer it would be before *they* got here.

'Who?' I meowed. 'Who *are* these people who need me to be shut in the house till they get here?'

The doorbell rang, and everyone seemed to jump. Julian marched to the front door with Caroline and Grace running behind him, and Laura took off her apron and picked Jessica up from the carpet. I scampered after everyone and Julian called to Caroline to hold me and stop me running out when he opened the door.

'Oh, hello!' He held the door open and Nicky walked in as we all stared at her as if she was a stranger. 'It's just Nicky,' he called back to Laura.

'Who were you expecting, then?' she said, laughing. 'The queen?'

'Not quite!' he said. 'Come in. Laura's in the lounge.'

'We're waiting for the TV people,' Caroline told her. 'They've come to make a film about Charlie.'

'It'll just be a little piece for the News, Caroline,' Julian warned her. 'Don't get too carried away.'

'Really? How exciting!' Nicky said. She smiled at Laura and Jessica as we all walked through to the lounge. 'It's actually Charlie I've come to tell you about,' she added as Caroline put me down on the sofa. 'You'll never guess what happened last night.'

'What?' Laura looked alarmed. 'He didn't get into a fight or anything, did he? He's only just been allowed out again. I didn't think he'd start going out at night so soon.'

'Nothing like that. He was out visiting Oliver at the pub, apparently – Dan saw them in there. And … well, this is going to sound really weird, but he says they made him come home.'

'*Made* him…?' Julian glanced at Laura, who glanced at me, frowned, and looked back at Nicky.

'How do you mean?' she said.

'I don't know. I think it must be Oliver. Daniel always did say he thought that cat had some special power to make him do things. But the thing is…' She sat down next to Laura, went a bit pink, and went on quietly, 'Well, the thing is, my next door neighbour had come in for a chat.'

'Not Kevin the Creep?' Laura said, laughing.

'Yes. Only it wasn't quite so funny anymore.' Nicky looked at Caroline and Grace now, then looked back at Laura, raising her eyebrows like it was some kind of code. 'He was being a bit too friendly. If you get my meaning.' The eyebrows again. It must have been human body language.

'What, was he coming on to you, Nicky?' Caroline said, nudging Grace, and they both started giggling.

Nicky went even pinker, and looked down at her lap.

'Oh my God,' Laura said. 'And Daniel came home just in the nick of time?'

'Yes, with the two cats! And as you can probably imagine, he was pretty upset.'

'Not with you, though, Nicky?' Julian said.

'No. He told me afterwards he'd overheard me telling Kevin to back off, that I wasn't interested. But Kevin started to argue the toss, and ... well, Dan got hold of him and nearly hit him.'

'Oh my God!' Laura said again, putting her hand to her mouth. Even Caroline and Grace had their mouths open wide with surprise, while Julian was trying to look serious.

'But he didn't, I hope?' he said.

'No.' Nicky glanced down at me again. 'But only because *this* little chap stopped him. It was unbelievable, honestly, you should have seen him. He threw himself at Dan and clung to his jacket by his claws, yowling at him. It brought Dan up short, and by the time he'd lifted Charlie off himself, he'd calmed down.'

'Oh my...' Laura just stopped herself from calling the God person yet again. She shook her head, and everyone in the room stared at me. I felt a bit self-conscious.

'Sorry!' I meowed. 'It just seemed like the right thing to do at the time. Ollie was proud of me.'

But it seemed like Ollie wasn't the only one.

'That's amazing,' Laura said, reaching for me and giving me a hug.

'Clever little Charlie,' Caroline said, coming over to stroke me. 'I *said* he was a hero, Daddy, didn't I?'

'Oh, come on! It was probably just a coincidence,' Julian said, shaking his head. 'He might have simply jumped up at Daniel to get a cuddle from him, and clung on with his claws to stop himself from falling.'

'You weren't there, Julian, with all due respect,' Nicky said quietly. 'You didn't see him.'

'And we should all know by now, cats *do* look after humans and try to help them,' Laura said. 'After all the things Oliver did last year to help our village. And particularly our family, Julian.'

They all went quiet for a minute, looking at each other. I knew what they were thinking about, of course, because I'd heard all about it from Oliver himself – how he'd visited Caroline, before I was born, when she was poorly and lonely because she had no friends. And also how he made Christmas better for everyone in the village.

'Yes. OK, Oliver did ... somehow ... seem to turn things around for us, didn't he,' he admitted. 'Perhaps you're right. Perhaps there's more goes on in a cat's mind than we can ever understand. But look at Charlie. He's only a little kitten, who ran away and got lost! I just can't quite believe ...'

'I am *not* a little kitten anymore,' I said crossly. 'Even Ollie admits that now.'

'Well, as far as I'm concerned,' Nicky said, 'Charlie and Oliver have saved my marriage. Daniel needed a sharp shock like that, to make him realise he was neglecting me and Benjamin. He got up early this morning to make Benny's breakfast, and as soon as he got back from doing a bit of work this morning, he's taken him out to the park in his buggy. He says he's going to advertise for another mechanic to work for him, and in the meantime he'll let the apprentice help a bit more where he can, so he's not so exhausted. He's been so focused on making the business a success, taking on all the work he could, and getting so tired, he admits he couldn't face coming home and helping with his own son. He just fell into the pub every night and then couldn't summon up the energy to come home. He knows he needs to make some changes and try to get some balance.'

'Good for him,' Laura said gently. 'I'm so glad you're going to work it out together.'

'Thanks to Charlie and Oliver,' Nicky insisted.

And before there could be any further discussion on the matter, at that moment the doorbell rang again – and this time, yes, it was the television people. And so we come to another chapter in my story!

CHAPTER
TWENTY ONE

It's getting a bit late. Is anyone too tired to hear the rest of my story now? No? Good, because we're almost up to date. We're nearly at the point where I found out all the answers. Not all the answers to everything in the world, of course, as I suppose that even for someone who isn't a little kitten anymore, there will always be things in the world that I don't understand. But after the television people came, I understood *some* things, at least. And later on, I understood a lot more.

I was shut in the lounge while they came into the house, in case I was daft enough to try to run off before I'd even been allowed to star in my own story. I listened from behind the closed door as the voices greeted each other, and finally the door was flung open and someone gasped:

'And is this our little hero?'

'If you say so!' I meowed, trotting up to the strangers to have a good sniff around their legs and see if they smelt friendly. A couple of them bent down to stroke me, and Caroline was being very jumpy with excitement, answering questions like was she pleased to have me back home, and how much did she miss me while I was gone? Then Julian took over, suggesting everyone sat down so they could talk properly, and Laura went to make tea and coffee.

'Charlie's story has really caught people's imaginations,' said a man called Andy who seemed to be in charge. 'They

267

loved the fact that a little cat like Charlie was brave enough to chase away a seagull and save an elderly lady from possible harm.'

'So everyone agrees it was definitely Charlie in that video?' Julian said.

'I think we can assume it,' Andy said. 'There were lots of witnesses, don't forget. And the two ladies ... um...' He glanced at a piece of paper in a folder that was open on his lap, 'Jean Francis and Shirley Benson, who found him, have said they're quite sure it was him. The cat in the video Shirley's niece made had the same bad eye and the same sore place on his leg and everything. Well, as you might know, there's been considerable nuisance in the Mudditon area recently from some particularly aggressive seagulls, and since Charlie's story broke, there's been a lot more discussion in the local press there, and on social media, about how to combat the problem to prevent their tourist industry suffering. It seems it's made local people, and holidaymakers, more aware of the need to dispose of food rubbish properly and not to feed the gulls with food meant for humans.'

'Let's hope it works, then,' Julian said. 'We were all very sorry to hear about tourism suffering in Mudditon.'

'Well, that'll be mentioned in this little follow-up film,' Andy said. 'It's been pointed out, too, that the local feral cats help the situation by keeping down the food waste themselves. And some of the witnesses to Charlie's little episode say there were feral cats hanging around behind him at the time.'

'Probably waiting to attack him, poor Charlie!' said Laura, who'd come back in now with the tray of coffee.

'No, we were working as a team!' I meowed, but as usual nobody was listening to me, even though I was supposed to be the hero.

'I don't know about that, of course,' Andy said. 'But according to our interviews with local people, gangs of feral cats had been seen chasing seagulls on several occasions around that time. It's quite unusual behaviour! But it seems there's been a change of attitude towards the cats in the town. They're being tolerated more, on the whole, and a couple of local fishermen even went on record saying they'd taken to throwing them the occasional fish.'

I was delighted to hear this. I purred happily to myself at the thought of Big and the others getting free fish at the harbour and not being shooed away so often by the humans.

'So what we'd like to do today,' Andy went on, 'is have a little chat with you all about Charlie – the background of how he went missing and how he was found. And of course we'll film some footage of him being happy back at home here with the family, so that everyone – all his fans! – can see how much better he's looking and how well he's settled back down with you. We'll add our own commentary with a recap of the seagull incident, reminding everyone about how he came to be so famous in the Mudditon area. And we'll include the interview with the woman and boy from the beach café, of course.'

There was a silence.

'What woman and boy?' Julian said.

'Which beach café?' Laura asked at the same time.

'Um...' Andy rummaged through his papers again. 'Stella Parkin, who runs the Seashells beach café at Salty Cove, just outside Mudditon – and her nephew Robbie who helps her ... did we not tell you about this?'

'No.' Julian shook his head. 'Was this the *new development* you mentioned on the phone? You said you'd fill us in today about it.'

'Sorry, yes, so I did.' He smiled around at us all, pausing as he looked at Grace, who I'd noticed had gone a bit pink in the face and was nudging Caroline and whispering to her.

'Is she the lady who helped us when Caroline got hurt?' Grace asked quietly. And when Andy nodded, she said, turning back to Caroline, 'You remember, Caro. She got the boy to call an ambulance, and persuaded us that you needed to go to hospital. She was really kind.'

'I don't really remember that,' Caroline said. 'It's all a bit of a blur.'

'Of course it is,' Laura soothed her. 'So what have these people got to do with Charlie's story, Andy?'

'She's convinced it was Charlie who alerted her to the accident,' he said.

'*What?*' Julian said, looking surprised. 'I can't see how. Charlie was found in the harbour area at Mudditon, not at Salty Cove. Sorry, but it could've been any little tabby cat, couldn't it?'

'But, Daddy, I told you I thought I saw him, didn't I?' Caroline yelled, so loudly that baby Jessica, sitting in her little bouncy seat next to the sofa, jumped and started to cry. 'I *knew* it was him. It's the only clear memory I've got, of that day, until I got to the hospital.'

'Yes, darling, but honestly, it isn't very likely, is it?'

As you can imagine, by now I was meowing for all I was worth, trying to tell them it was true, it was me, I'd been there, I'd tried to help!

'Actually, Mr Smythe, there are photos,' Andy said. 'Would you like to see them?'

'Well, yes, of course, but how...?' Julian was saying, looking confused, as Andy rummaged through his folder again.

'Robbie from the café took some pictures of the cat on his phone. His aunt apparently took the cat in to give him some food and milk, after the girls were taken to hospital,' Andy explained. He chuckled. 'Stella said in our interview that he's never off the phone, using Twitter and WhatsApp and so on while he's supposed to be working. Well, he shared these photos on his social media accounts as usual. Apparently he told Stella he was doing it to try to find the cat's owner. But instead he made a joke of it, saying his aunt thought this cat had told her about an accident on the beach. He thought it was funny, said he thought she was barmy. But a couple of weeks later, when the networks started buzzing with pictures of the incident in Mudditon with the seagull, he looked at them and thought it could actually be the same cat. He showed his aunt, and she was convinced it was. After we ran our first news story, she contacted us to tell us about *her* experience.' He held out a couple of pictures to Julian. 'Printouts of the nephew's shots,' he said. 'What do you think?'

Well, everyone in the room now nearly fell over each other to get to the pictures. I tried to get a look myself, but they were all in my way.

'I remember the boy holding his phone up at me,' I meowed. I knew this made pictures appear. Were these the pictures? Were they pictures of me?

'Let me see!' Caroline was squealing.

'Is it him?' Laura said, looking excited.

'Oh my God, Caro,' Grace said. 'Maybe it really was Charlie!'

Julian was the only one staying quiet. He held the pictures, staring at them, one after the other, with Caroline leaning on the back of the sofa, looking over his shoulder.

'It's him, Daddy, I know it is,' she said. She sounded like she was about to start mewing. 'Charlie came to my rescue! He saw me getting hurt, and went to get the lady from the café.'

'It *could* be him,' Julian said, sounding a bit less doubtful now. 'What do you think, Laura?' He passed her the pictures, and she looked at them with Nicky.

'I think it is him,' Laura said. 'It's how he looked before, Julian – before he got into the fight, or got attacked, or whatever, and got the injuries. Before he lost weight and everything.'

'But why would he have been at Salty Cove?' Nicky said.

'He must have followed us,' Grace said.

'Yes, he must have done,' Caroline agreed. 'If he ran out of the house when we opened the door, then he must have trailed us all the way we walked that night, Grace, without us seeing him.'

'Yes, and ... oh my God, he must've seen us go in the beach hut, and ... waited around outside all night,' Grace said. 'And then he saw what happened on the beach in the morning.'

'Yes!' I meowed. I jumped off Caroline's lap and scampered around the room, doing a few little jumps of excitement so that they all laughed at me. 'That's what happened. But what I *don't* know is what happened after you went off in the ambulance. Nobody's told me.'

And it looked like nobody was going to, either. They were much too busy discussing the mystery (to them) of how I ended up back at Mudditon. Hello? I walked! It wasn't very far, along the coast. Shouldn't they have known that, if they were so clever? And then they were listening to Andy telling them how the film was going to be put together, with the café lady's story, and Jean and Shirley's story, as well as my family talking about me and their relief about having me back home.

When they were all ready, Andy held up a thing called a microphone and started talking to Caroline and Grace, while his friend Sandeep was filming them on his huge camera. By then, I'd finally begun to understand how I got inside the television that first time, because Sandeep had spent a while showing the girls the camera, playing back a bit of film to them. Because I was sitting on Caroline's lap at the time, I could see that it did the same thing as their phones did when they filmed each other. And Sandeep explained that these moving pictures would eventually appear on people's television screens. I can't say it makes sense to me, any more than lots of the weird things humans do. But now I see there is some kind of connection between cameras or phones, and televisions, so maybe it isn't actually magic.

It was nice being cuddled on Caroline's lap while Andy talked to her about what happened in Mudditon. Because Julian had already warned him that the girls had been punished enough for running away, and he didn't want it brought up again, Andy just referred to it as their *little adventure that went wrong*.

'Charlie must have come with us, and followed us,' Caroline said into the microphone. 'We didn't realise.'

'But it seems it was a good thing he did,' Andy said. 'And when you and Grace got lost, he seems to have stood guard over you all night.'

'Well, to be quite honest I fell asleep under a bench,' I meowed. But Caroline stroked me and said yes, I must have been protecting them, which made me feel a bit guilty.

'So can you tell us what happened the next morning?' Andy asked, and Grace explained how the seagull swooped on their sandwiches and bit Caroline's finger.

'I tried to run off, and I must have tripped on the rocks,' Caroline said. 'I don't really remember it very well.'

'She hit her head, cut it open, and knocked herself out,' Grace said.

'That must have been very frightening,' Andy said. 'And it seems that's when Charlie managed to get the attention of Stella at the café.'

'Yes, that lady was very kind, and she said the boy had called an ambulance,' Grace said.

'And what a good job you were taken to hospital, Caroline,' Julian said, sounding very serious.

I looked around the room. Everyone was much more serious now. Caroline was looking down at the floor and Laura reached out to put a paw on her arm.

'Perhaps your dad would like to explain what happened, Caroline,' Andy said, and the camera turned towards Julian.

'Well, we'd been frantic with worry, of course,' he said, 'so when we got a call to say the girls were at the hospital, we – and Grace's parents – rushed straight there. And Caroline—'

He broke off, swallowing hard. I looked up at him. Caroline what?

'She looked dreadful,' he said very quietly, 'and there were doctors all round her. We … well, as you can probably imagine, we didn't know what to think.'

'We feared the worst,' Laura said. 'She'd been very ill, you see, and we were still waiting for results of a biopsy, to see whether there was a recurrence of her illness. So we were very, very worried at that point.'

'They told us she'd had an accident, and at first all we could see was a wound on her finger,' Julian said. 'But she was so pale, and she kept complaining of a headache and feeling sick and dizzy.'

'And she seemed quite confused,' Laura added. 'She wasn't too sure where she was, or what had happened.'

'And then, of course, the doctor showed us where she'd hit the back of her head when she fell, and that Grace had told them she'd been unconscious, so they were treating it as concussion,' Julian said. 'But when we told them about the leukaemia, and the fact that we'd been worried about her health recently, they obviously took that very seriously. And, well, to cut a long story short, if she hadn't been taken straight to hospital, the concussion could have been missed, which could have had really serious consequences in itself. We might have thought her symptoms were linked to the ... other health worries, you see.' He shook his head. 'It really doesn't bear thinking about.'

'So it seems your little cat actually saved the day!' Andy said, beaming at me.

'If it really was Charlie who alerted someone to call an ambulance, then I'd say...' Julian was looking at me too now, with a strange expression on his face, 'to be honest, he could have actually saved her life.'

CHAPTER
TWENTY TWO

Finally, they believed me. I'd rescued the girls! And not only that, I'd saved Caroline's life. This called for a celebration. With a little meow of happiness, I hopped up onto Andy's lap, knocked the pen out of his paw (I do like a nice pen to play with), and jumped back down after it, batting it along the floor with my paws and leaping around, pretending it was a mouse. For a minute, everyone stayed quiet, watching me – and then they all burst out laughing at once, with the man called Andy going into a real frenzy of excitement.

'Did you get that?' he demanded of Sandeep, who'd now turned off the camera for a moment. 'And the looks on all their faces? Great! This is fantastic. What a story! It's even better than I thought it was going to be. It's going to go national. The human interest factor – the kitten who saved a life! I mean, it's like, wow!' He waved his paws about, grinning all over his face. I stared at him. He was talking in that funny way Caroline did when she was with her friends!

But then, all of a sudden, he stopped, went very quiet, and said:

'Oh my God, I'm so sorry. How very inappropriate of me. I mean, in view of Caroline's condition . . .' He glanced at Caroline and lowered his voice even more. 'The leukaemia?'

'Exactly what I was thinking,' I meowed. I mean – were they *ever* going to tell me whether she was all right?

'Oh sorry,' Laura said. 'We didn't finish explaining.' She paused for a moment, as if she was thinking about what to say, then went on, 'You see, when we told the doctor at the Mudditon hospital that we were still waiting for biopsy results from London, he got straight on the phone to them, and then came back saying it was negative. No abnormal cells found. It seems there's no recurrence of the leukaemia.'

'Phew,' Andy said. 'I'm very glad to hear that.'

Me too! At last, I'd found out what I needed to know. Caroline wasn't ill after all. Everything was all right with the world! I'd got back on her lap by now, bored with the pen, so I gave her face a good licking, making her giggle.

But then I thought again about how tired and pale she looked, how worried Julian and Laura still looked when they kept asking her if she was OK. Something didn't seem right. What were they still not telling me? Or were they just *pretending* to Andy that she was OK? I mewed to myself a bit, feeling anxious all over again.

I looked at Julian and Laura now, and felt even more anxious when I saw they were frowning at each other, and Julian was shaking his head like he didn't want her to say any more. As usual, humans, with their rubbish body language, made it impossible to understand what they were thinking. Surely, I told myself, Laura wouldn't have said Caroline didn't have the illness, if she did? Surely, if she did have it, she'd be going back to the hospital, instead of going to school? I just had to believe what Laura said, didn't I?

By now Andy and Sandeep had turned off the camera and the microphone things, and all the adults were just carrying on chatting, so it seemed I wasn't needed anymore. Perhaps it would be best to try to take my mind off my worries. I jumped down from Caroline's lap again and went over to have a sniff around some of their equipment.

'We'll pack up and get away now, then. Thanks for everything,' Andy said after they'd chatted for a while longer. It was a bit embarrassing, because I'd somehow got myself tangled up in some leads for the camera. At first I thought it was good fun, playing with their stuff while they weren't looking, but when they wanted to start packing things away I couldn't get myself out of the mess I'd made, and they had to unravel me. Andy wasn't cross though.

'He's such a cute little cat,' he laughed. I couldn't help thinking about how I used to get told off if I got tangled up in Laura's washing. Although that was before I went missing. She didn't seem to get so stern with me these days.

'This is going to be such a great little story,' Andy said again as they finally headed for the door.

'Good. And if the publicity helps the campaign in Mudditon – getting people to alter their behaviour with regard to the seagulls – it'll be worth it,' Julian said.

'Yes. Nothing wrong with seagulls in their place, is there, but their place isn't being fed human food and attacking people to get it,' Andy agreed. 'Well, Charlie, you're already a hero to the people in Mudditon, and now you're a hero to your family as well,' he said, giving me a stroke. 'They must be so proud of you, little kitten.'

'*Not* a little kitten!' I meowed crossly at him. 'For mewing out loud, look at me, I'm a grown-up cat now.'

Although, to be fair, I suppose if I'd been so very grown up I might not have got tangled in the wires.

Nicky stayed for a while longer after the television people left. Caroline and Grace went off to play in her bedroom.

'It was good to see Caroline looking happy and excited,' Laura said after the three of them had sat in silence for a while.

'You're still worried about her, aren't you?' Nicky said. 'I must admit, she does still look pale.'

'Oh, Nicky, we just don't know what to think!' Laura sounded like she was almost mewing, and Julian, who was holding her paw now, was staring at the carpet. I'd been washing myself in a corner of the room, but as you can imagine, I sat up and listened again. 'We keep telling ourselves it's just tiredness, you know, because of the new school,' she went on.

'Or even the after-effects of the concussion,' Julian put in. 'They did warn us at the hospital that she might still suffer from headaches, dizziness and difficulty in concentrating – for as long as three months after the accident.'

'And are those the sort of symptoms she's complaining about?' Nicky asked quietly.

'Well, she's not really complaining much at all, bless her,' Laura said. 'Not since Charlie came home, anyway – she's

282

so thrilled to have him back. But she does admit she's really tired all the time. And you've seen how she's looking, Nicky. You can understand why we're finding it so difficult not to be worried still.'

'Perhaps it's only natural that you'll always worry about her? After what she went through before,' Nicky said.

'Maybe. But … well, I'm thinking we should take her back to our own doctor. Just to make sure,' Julian said, glancing at Laura as he said it.

'It can't hurt, can it? Just for your own peace of mind?' Nicky said.

'Julian's worried they might have got the biopsy result wrong,' Laura said, in such a soft little voice I almost missed it. She had her paw over her mouth, as if she didn't really want the words to come out. 'I keep telling him how unlikely that is, but…'

'But we need to be sure,' Julian said in a much louder, firmer voice. 'I can't go on like this, Laura, on edge all the time, wondering. If there's been a mistake, we need to know.'

'I'm sure there hasn't,' Nicky said, a little wobble in her voice. 'But I agree, if you're that worried, you should get her checked out again.' She got up and gave them both a hug. 'Please let me know, won't you? Dan and I are worried too – about all of you.'

By now I was pacing the floor back and forth, mewing to myself, with all the excitement of the day forgotten. It was all very well being told I'd saved Caroline's life – but if it still turned out that she was seriously ill, then perhaps I hadn't done enough life-saving, after all.

*

283

I didn't sleep very well that night, and when Oliver came to see me the next morning, to tell me that he'd actually managed to get some news about Caroline, at first I couldn't quite take in what he was saying.

'What do you mean?' I asked, still thinking about what I'd heard the previous day. 'You're not a human doctor, all of a sudden, are you?'

'Human doctor?' He stared at me. 'What are you talking about, and why are you being so tetchy? I promised you I'd listen in on Nicky and Daniel's conversations, didn't I?'

'Oh. Yes, sorry. What have you heard?'

'Well, please don't get too upset. But I heard Nicky telling Daniel that your owners are going to take Caroline back to the doctors because they're still worried she might be ill again.'

'Oh, yes, I know that.'

'You do?'

'Yes, it came up yesterday when Nicky was here.' I rubbed my face against his. 'I'm sorry, Ollie, I'm so worried about Caroline myself now, I can't think straight.'

'I know. I was pretty worried when I heard the news. Is there anything I can do? Shall I stay and play with you for a while to cheer you up?'

'If you don't mind, I think I'd rather be on my own with the family.'

'Of course.' He looked so sad, it made me feel guilty, but it was no good – I just couldn't get myself back out of the black mood that had come over me. It wasn't until he'd gone that I realised I hadn't even told him about the

TV people, and about being called a hero and a life-saver. It just didn't seem so important or clever anymore.

Julian told Caroline that evening about going back to the doctor's in the morning. I was lying on the rug next to baby Jessica, tickling her with my tail and my whiskers to make her giggle. Even the fact that Laura wasn't telling me off anymore about the possibility of germs, was making me sad, because she looked so anxious and distracted, it felt like I could have sat right on Jessica's head and she still wouldn't have reacted. Not that I was going to do it, of course. I really loved little Jessica these days.

'Oh,' was all Caroline said about the doctor's. We all waited for her to start protesting and complaining about it, but she didn't, and in a way that was worse.

'It's just a precaution, Caroline,' Laura said. 'We're sure there's nothing to worry about, but you must admit, you've been so tired all the time.'

'Yes,' she said.

'It's probably the after-effects of the concussion,' Julian said.

'Or even just the new school,' Laura joined in. I got the impression they were both trying to sound cheerful. 'You know, the longer day, the extra work, carrying all those books...'

'Yes.'

'So that's probably what the doctor will say,' Laura went on.

'But we just thought we'd make sure,' said Julian.

There was a long silence, during which Caroline came and lay down on the floor next to me, and started playing with me and Jessica.

'OK,' she said eventually. 'Can you make the appointment for after school? Otherwise I'll have to have a note.'

I worried all the next day. I almost couldn't eat my lunch. When Laura finally came home after the doctor's appointment I was so relieved that Caroline was with her, and hadn't been taken straight to the hospital, I purred all round her legs for ages while she sat at the table having milk and biscuits. But it wasn't until Julian came home from work that I found anything out.

'Dr Pearson says the bone marrow biopsy looks conclusive,' she said. 'He's sure there's no mistake. I asked him whether he thought we ought to repeat it just in case.' She glanced at Caroline. Again, I was expecting her to howl in protest, but she just sat there, listening, playing with the thing that turns the TV on and off.

'And?' Julian asked anxiously.

'Well, he said he'd like to get a couple more ordinary blood tests done first, to check for other possible reasons, before we go down that road.'

'What sort of other reasons? Did he agree that it might be because of the concussion?'

'He did seem to consider it. But he said there could be any number of reasons – it was like he didn't want to commit himself until we've got the results of the blood tests. So I'm taking Caroline to the health clinic in Great

Broomford for those, first thing in the morning. Dr Pearson will have the results by Wednesday.'

Those next two days seemed twice as long as normal. I almost couldn't eat my breakfast, lunch *or* dinner. I tried to keep myself busy by amusing Jessica, by chasing birds in the garden and playing in the fallen leaves, but nothing seemed to work. When Oliver called round I was almost too anxious to meow with him at all, let alone start telling him the story of my time in Mudditon. When Caroline came home from school on Wednesday afternoon, Laura was waiting for her with Jessica already in her car seat, to take her straight back to the doctor's. They went off without even saying goodbye to me. I meowed at them from the window as Laura drove away, but I knew it was because, like me, they couldn't think of anything apart from the test results. They were gone for so long, Julian got home from work before they returned.

'Why are they taking so long, eh, Charlie?' he asked, bending down to stroke my head.

'I wish I knew,' I meowed.

'I'll try calling Laura's phone,' he said, and I sat up straight in my bed, watching him as he held the phone to his ear. Laura must have answered quickly, because the next thing he said was: '*Where*? The supermarket? Why the hell … Laura, I'm sitting here worrying myself sick, waiting for you to come home. At least tell me what the doctor said.'

Then he frowned, said 'OK. Yes. See you in a bit, then.' And, turning to me, he added, 'She can't even talk to me right now, because she's at the checkout. Honestly, Charlie – women! What a time to choose to go shopping.'

I agreed. I mean, I realised it was obviously necessary to stock up on my cat food, but I'd have thought it could have waited till the morning. Julian made himself a cup of coffee and we both settled down to wait. And I tried not to wonder whether Laura had taken Caroline shopping to cheer her up – because they'd had bad news.

CHAPTER
TWENTY THREE

It was only a little while before we heard Laura's car pull up outside. Julian got up and went to the front door. He was so agitated, he was doing a little dance from one foot to the other on the doorstep, and I walked round and round his feet, feeling exactly the same.

'Hello!' Laura called out cheerfully as she carried Jessica out of the car.

She didn't sound at all upset. Or was she just pretending to be cheerful for Caroline's sake? But then Caroline came bounding up to the door behind her, smiling and saying she was hungry. That was a good sign, surely? I never looked forward to the arguments and sulks at dinnertime, or Laura's sighs and downturned mouth when Caroline left half her dinner on the plate. Perhaps if she was saying she was hungry, she might eat it all up and everyone would be happy. Just as long as she wasn't ill.

'What took you so long?' Julian asked as we all went through to the kitchen. 'I've been on edge here for ages, waiting to hear what the doctor said.'

'Sorry. We needed a few bits of shopping,' Laura said, putting a bulging carrier bag on the kitchen table. 'Have you got the other bag, Caroline?'

'Yes, here you go.' She deposited another bulging carrier bag next to the first one, and they smiled at each other.

'What's going on?' Julian said, looking bewildered, and I didn't blame him. It was beginning to look like the shopping was more important than the visit to the doctor.

'We'll explain in a minute. Just put the kettle on first, would you? I'm gasping for a cup of tea. And Jessica's nappy needs changing. I'll do that while you make the tea.'

She carried Jessica off upstairs, and Julian, shaking his head, turned to put the kettle on and get out mugs and tea bags, while Caroline rummaged in the cupboard for a biscuit.

'You know Laura's rules,' Julian warned her. 'No snacks just before dinner. You leave half your meals, as it is.'

'I won't tonight, though,' she said, grinning.

Julian sat down opposite her at the table, staring at her.

'Is there some kind of secret going on that I'm not being allowed to share?' he asked her, a bit crossly. 'All I want to know is what the doctor said about the blood tests, and whether you're OK.'

'Sorry, Dad.' Caroline reached across the table and touched his paw. 'I know you've been worried. So have I. But it's OK. I don't need another bone marrow biopsy. It's nothing serious.'

'So what *is* it?'

'Anaemia,' Laura said, suddenly reappearing in the kitchen doorway. 'That's what's been wrong with her, Julian, and it's all my fault.'

'No it's not,' Caroline said. 'It's my fault, Laura. If I didn't want to eat meat, I should have researched it myself, shouldn't I, to find out what I should eat, instead of just having tantrums about it like a baby.'

'It's because she hasn't been eating meat?' Julian said, looking from Caroline to Laura and back again, his eyebrows right up to the top of his head. 'That's why she's been so tired and unwell?'

'No. Not exactly.' Laura sighed and sat down at the table next to him. 'It's not the lack of meat in itself – Dr Pearson says a vegetarian diet can be very healthy if it's done properly. No, it's the lack of anything sensible in her diet *instead* of meat. And that *is* my fault. I've been too busy trying to get Caroline to eat what *I* wanted her to eat, to think about what nutrients she might be missing. And I'm a nurse! I feel so stupid.'

'Laura, you've been really busy since Jessica was born,' Caroline said quietly. 'And I know I was being difficult about it. The thing is, I just really hate the whole idea of eating dead animals! I'd been feeling like this about it for a long time, ever since I was ill I suppose, but I didn't really *want* to be awkward and difficult. I did keep trying to eat some meat, but then it started making me feel really sick.' She shrugged. 'Perhaps you're right, Laura – it might just be a phase, maybe I'll get over it.'

'It doesn't matter anymore, Caroline,' Laura said. 'I'm just glad we've found out what's wrong.'

'So what does Dr Pearson suggest? Iron tablets?' Julian asked.

'Not unless we can't correct it ourselves with diet.'

'What sort of diet?'

'Look in the bags, Dad!' Caroline said, sounding quite excited as she started to unpack the two carriers, describing each item as she put it on the table 'Lots of green veg. Dried apricots. Lentils. Soya beans. Tofu. Oatmeal. Cashew nuts. Sunflower seeds—'

'And lots of oranges, strawberries, blackcurrants and so on, for vitamin C,' Laura put in.

'Because, did you know? We need vitamin C in order to absorb iron,' Caroline said, sounding quite excited about it.

'And plenty of cheese of course, and yoghurts and eggs. For protein.'

All this sounded awful to me, but Laura and Caroline were grinning away to each other happily.

'Caroline has really taken it on board,' Laura said. 'She wanted us to go straight to the supermarket and stock up on all the right food, so that we can start today.'

'Are you sure you're up for this?' Julian said, sounding worried again now. 'It sounds like a lot of work, Laura – two different meals every night? I mean, you know I'd help, but I normally get home a bit late…'

Laura laughed. 'Don't worry, I'm not expecting you to learn vegetarian cooking, Julian.'

'But *I'm* going to,' Caroline said, sitting up a bit straighter. 'That's only fair, if I want to eat differently from you, isn't it? And anyway I think it's really interesting. I can cook stir fries with lots of nuts, and make lentil bakes, and…'

'We picked up a recipe book in the supermarket too,' Laura told Julian.

'And I'm going to start on tonight's dinner as soon as I've changed out of my school uniform,' Caroline said, running off towards the stairs.

'I do realise the novelty of cooking for herself will probably wear off after a while,' Laura said, smiling at Julian. 'And I'll supervise anyway. But it won't do her any harm. We can both learn, together. I don't think it's going to be as difficult as it sounds. We might even decide to join her, a couple of days a week. Too much meat is bad for you, you know,' she added.

Really? I found that hard to believe. I couldn't imagine how anyone could survive without eating meat. Even when I was living in such reduced circumstances with the feral cats, it was the scraps of horrible burgers and sausages from the bins, together with the occasional treat of fresh fish of course, that kept us alive. But to be honest I was just so very, very happy to hear that Caroline wasn't really ill after all, I didn't care what strange things she wanted to eat, as long as they made her feel better.

'Dr Pearson also reminded me that she's approaching puberty,' Laura added quietly, 'which, as well as the anaemia, would account for her having been so tired and emotional.' She paused for a moment, and then smiled and said, 'And moody, and bad-tempered!'

I was glad poor Caroline wasn't in the room to hear that.

'Really? She's at that stage already? She's only eleven!'

'Coming up for twelve,' Laura said. 'It's not at all out of the ordinary, Julian. I should have realised that myself, but I kind of expected that she'd have a slightly delayed adolescence, if anything, after going through her illness and the chemotherapy. But the doctor said that doesn't necessarily happen.'

'The trouble is, we've both been seeing all the signs, but thinking they meant something else. Something much worse. So we couldn't see the wood for the trees.'

'Yes, you're right. Well – thank God, she's going to be fine now.' Laura reached out and touched Julian's paw. 'It's such a relief, isn't it?'

A relief to me too, of course. In fact I felt quite weak with it. I was going to have to have a lie down. But first, I needed to wind myself around Caroline's legs until she picked me up, so that I could give her face a really good licking to show how happy I was.

Later that night, after Jessica had gone to bed and Caroline had gone back upstairs to do her homework, Nicky came round. Apparently she'd been desperate to hear how the doctor's appointment went, too.

'I'm so glad it's nothing serious,' she said after Laura had told her all about it. 'So it's nothing to do with the new school, either? I was a bit worried she was finding it too much.'

'No, she absolutely loves the school,' Julian said. 'And we're both completely certain now that we've done the right thing, aren't we, darling?'

Laura nodded. 'She's so happy at Great Broomford High, going off on the bus with all her friends, and being in the same class as Grace. And it is a good school, so I'm sure she'll do well there. Thank goodness there was still a place available for her there when we changed our minds.'

'Yes,' said Julian. 'If only we'd sat down and talked to her about it properly, instead of just insisting we knew what was best for her. The private school might have a wonderful reputation, but what's the point, if she was going to be miserable and resentful? Now she's got her circle of friends here, after all that time of being lonely, it's quite understandable that the most important thing for her is to be with them. No wonder she felt so cross and upset with us.'

'But she's happy now, and she's going to be fine, that's what matters,' Nicky said gently. 'What about the concussion, though? Did the doctor say that wasn't causing her any of her symptoms?'

'Oh, he did say it might be adding to the problem, yes,' Laura said, 'although the anaemia is the real issue. But I must say, he agreed with what they told us at Mudditon Hospital – if Caroline hadn't been taken to hospital, it could have been a different picture altogether. Can you imagine what might have happened if she and Grace had carried on wandering off on their own like that – while she was suffering from concussion, not to mention the bleeding from her wounds? It could have been … well, a catastrophe,' she finished in a very quiet voice.

'Thank God she went to hospital. So it looks like Charlie really *did* save her life,' Nicky said.

'Yes.' Laura looked at me and smiled. 'He did.'

'It feels like we've got our Caroline back now, in more ways than one,' Julian said, and I thought I could hear a funny wobble in his voice. Laura must have heard it too, because she put her paws round him and hugged him. He smiled at her and added, 'And *you're* so much happier too, darling, aren't you? Now the baby's started to settle down.'

'Poor Laura was tired out, Julian,' Nicky said. 'What on earth did you expect?'

'You were worried I might have had postnatal depression, weren't you?' Laura said, turning to Julian. 'But Nicky's right, I was just completely exhausted.'

'Men just don't get it,' Nicky said, shaking her head. 'Dan was absolutely useless too, after I had Benjamin.'

'I know, I know,' Julian said, smiling. 'Well, we don't like to admit we're worried, you see...'

'Excuses, excuses.' Nicky laughed. 'You're all the same. If you don't like us being tired and ratty, you should be looking at how you can help us. And honestly, Julian – I'm glad we're close enough friends that I can say this to you now – it really wasn't the most wonderful idea in the world, taking the family to Mudditon for a whole month and leaving them there to get on with it.'

Oh, at last, somebody was saying what we'd all been thinking right from the start! I rubbed my head against Nicky's legs and purred.

'I know,' Julian said. 'I think I realised I'd messed up, even before we got there, but I was trying to convince myself it was going to somehow make everything better. Instead, I'll admit it, it was just a bloody disaster!'

'Oh, come on, there were some good things about the holiday,' Laura said, nudging Nicky and doing that thing with her eyes that humans call winking. 'It was quite fun really apart from the girls running away, Charlie going missing, Caroline getting herself concussed and carted off to hospital, and ... oh, well, none of us being able to relax on the beach because of the seagulls. But that pales into insignificance compared with the rest!'

'Next year,' Julian said, when they'd all stopped laughing, '*you* choose the holiday, right? That's a promise.'

'And Charlie can stay with us,' Nicky said firmly. 'Wherever you go, you're not going to risk taking him with you again and letting him get lost.'

'You're on,' Laura said. 'Thank you. The cattery is supposed to be very good, though.'

'No!' I meowed. 'I want to stay with Nicky. I'll be really, really good! I won't mess up her washing or get inside Benjamin's cot or anything.'

'I think he's saying he'd rather stay with us,' Nicky said, stroking me. Perhaps she actually did understand a bit of Cat!

'Well, next summer's a long way off,' Julian said, 'but we might take you up on it if Laura wants us to jet off somewhere exotic and expensive.'

'Good idea!' Laura said, and she did the winking thing to Nicky again. 'Although to be honest, I can't imagine exotic holidays being quite so easy with a baby in tow. And it's funny, but despite everything, I've developed a kind of affection for Mudditon-on-Sea.'

'You're joking!' Julian said.

'No, I'm not. But we're only going back if they've got a grip on the seagull problem. And as long as it's only for a week or two, *and* you stay with us.'

'Perhaps we could stay in a hotel next time instead of self-catering,' Julian said. 'And we'll see if Grace can come along for Caroline.'

Nicky was laughing at them both as she got to her feet. 'Well, I'd better get back or Dan's going to start complaining that *I* leave *him* on his own too much with Benjamin! I'll leave the pair of you to mull over your plans for next year, then – although I can hardly believe you're already talking about going back to Mudditon again.'

And neither could I. After everything that happened, here they were already discussing going on another holiday! What on earth is wrong with humans? Why can't they just enjoy playing in their own safe territories all the time, like we do? Although I must admit, just for a tiny moment, I allowed myself to imagine going back to Mudditon and somehow being able to catch up with my friends, the feral cats, again. But sadly, I knew it wasn't really going to happen. I'll never forget those boys, but they're not part of my real life, my life here in Little Broomford with my family and friends. I'm a home-loving domestic cat at heart, and always will be.

After Nicky left, I took myself off to my bed in the kitchen to settle down for the night, but I couldn't sleep for thinking about all the things I'd overheard. Suddenly there was a rattle of the cat flap and there was Oliver looking through it. I jumped up at once and dived outside to join him.

'What have you been doing?' he complained. 'I've been meowing outside for you for ages, but you've obviously been too busy to hear me.'

'Sorry,' I said. 'It's been a very worrying day. Caroline went back to the doctor to find out whether she's ill again.'

'Oh yes! What happened?'

'She's OK.' I felt almost too tired to explain. 'But she has to eat strange things like nuts and eggs and oranges.'

'Yuck. Poor Caroline.'

'I know, but we're all really happy because she's going to be fine.'

'Of course. I'm happy about it too.' He rubbed his face against mine. 'It's really good news. Thank goodness she's not ill. So – now we know that, if I come back tomorrow perhaps you'll finally tell me your story?'

'Yes. And I didn't tell you the other day about the television people coming—'

'*What?*'

'They want to put me into everyone's televisions again. They're calling me a hero.'

He gave me a funny look. 'Really? Don't start getting big ideas about yourself, Charlie. You're still just a little kitten to me, you know.'

And although it usually annoys me now, there was something quite comforting then about Ollie calling me a little kitten 'Don't worry. I won't get big-headed. But it turns out they're saying I saved Caroline's life.'

'Wow. Really?'

'Yes, and in Mudditon where we went on holiday, the humans think I was a hero because I saved an old female from being attacked by seagulls.'

'I can't wait to hear about all this. And of course, Charlie, we're both heroes for saving Nicky and Daniel's marriage as well.'

301

'Yes. I'm getting a bit tired actually, doing all this heroism and saving. I was just about to go to sleep before you turned up.'

'Oh, well, if you're too tired to talk to me…'

'Of course I'm not. Anyway, I couldn't get off to sleep. I was too excited about Caroline not being ill. And too busy puzzling about things my family have just been saying, as well.'

'Tell me about it!' he meowed. 'Humans puzzle me all the time. They're just not like us, you know.'

'I realise that. But whatever possesses them to want to go away on holidays? It's crazy. Once you start wandering away from home, trust me, Ollie, I've discovered life is fraught with dangers and difficulties. Personally, nothing will ever tempt me to do it again. Oh, unless, of course, I should ever be needed for another rescue of Caroline.'

'I can understand that. Adult humans should be able to look after themselves, but human kittens are pretty vulnerable. Especially when they're very small, like your Jessica, for instance.'

'Oh my claws and whiskers, that's a point! You're right, Jessica's a *really* tiny human kitten. So far, she can hardly move at all on her own. Everyone got all amazed and excited the other day just because she rolled over on the carpet, can you believe? She certainly won't be going anywhere far like that! But if she starts wandering when she's big enough, I'll have to start looking out for her, too, for sure. My work as a life-saving hero is obviously going to be an ongoing occupation. I feel exhausted just thinking about it.'

'Well, you'd better get your rest while you can, you poor exhausted life-saving hero!' he said. He sounded just a little bit sarcastic, I have to say, although not in a nasty way. Ollie would never be nasty to me. He just keeps me in my place, and I suppose that's fair enough.

'Are you sure you don't want to stay and hear some of my story now?'

'No. Tomorrow will be better. Quite frankly you look worn out. And anyway, I've been thinking. Some of the other cats in the village keep asking me if I know what happened to you while you were missing. Why don't you tell us all, together? I'll spread the word tonight, and we can meet by the dustbins round the back of the shop early in the morning.'

'You really think they'll be interested?'

'Oh yes, definitely.' He gave me a friendly rub with his face. 'I'm absolutely certain they'll all be agog to hear about the exploits of our local life-saving hero!'

And perhaps he was being a bit sarcastic again. But judging by the way you've all hung around to hear this story right to the very end, you know what? I think he might have been right. What's that, Tabitha? You don't want the story to end? Well, I'm sorry, but I'm pretty sure it must be nearly dinnertime again. And even heroes like me need to eat, you know. We all need to keep our strength up, just in case.

Just in case what? Well, who knows? Who knows when you might be called upon to save someone's life, just for instance? If it can happen to an ordinary little kitten like

I recently used to be, well, it could happen to any cat, anywhere. Be warned. Be prepared. Humans need us! Even if they don't realise it, they do, because let's face it, we're the superior race by far.

ACKNOWLEDGEMENTS

With grateful thanks to Sharon Whelan, Clinical Director at Clarendon House Vet's in Galleywood, Chelmsford, for advice on Charlie's care after his injuries.

And thanks to everyone at Ebury who helps with the process of turning my stories into proper books – with particular thanks to my editor Emily Yau for all her hard work on Charlie's behalf. Meow!